ALMOST

AMI RAO

Inspired by the extraordinary mind
of Roland Barthes

FAIRLIGHT BOOKS

First published by Fairlight Books 2022

Fairlight Books
Summertown Pavilion, 18–24 Middle Way, Oxford, OX2 7LG

A CIP catalogue record for this book is available from the British
Library

1 2 3 4 5 6 7 8 9 10

ISBN 978-1-912054-33-6

www.fairlightbooks.com

Printed and bound in Great Britain

Designed by Fairlight Books

This is a work of fiction. With the exception of any public figures,
names, characters, business, events and incidents are the products of
the author's imagination. Any resemblance to actual persons, living or
dead, or actual events is purely coincidental.

For my children

'When he shall die,
Take him and cut him out in little stars,
And he will make the face of heaven so fine
That all the world will be in love with night
And pay no worship to the garish sun.'
—William Shakespeare, *Romeo and Juliet*

Prologue

The wing of the death angel brushed against her wrist as she stood in the open doorway of the bus.

The girl with the auburn hair looked around, then seeing nothing that could possibly have touched her, frowned momentarily before she jumped off behind the others. The doors closed behind her with a series of short, staccato beeps. She watched as the bus pulled away and then disappeared down the A-road in a thick cloud of fog, only the back lights visible – glowing, phosphorescent eyes.

Already, she had forgotten about that cold feeling on her arm.

Six miles away, Paul William Sullivan stared sadly out of his car window. He hated the cold, hated the whole concept of winter, hated the rain, hated driving in the rain, but more than all of that, he hated the fact that he probably wouldn't have been driving in this – this freak show from heaven – if the skinny brunette sitting in her sun-filled office in Orlando with the spooky black cat on her lap hadn't rambled on like a cargo train with no brakes.

The bitch of the matter was that on *this* end, they had all dutifully gathered around the table in the little conference room on the fourth floor at 3.55pm – five minutes early. At 4.10pm – a whole ten minutes late – her pale, skinny, heart-shaped face had appeared on the screen. No apology, nothing. And then, waffling on like that about the cultural differences between breakfast foods in the developed West versus certain other parts of the world in her nasal voice with no regard to Greenwich and time zones and time-to-go-home-in-certain-other-parts-of-the-world-hello? The whole thing was meant to last an hour. But no. No such luck in Paul W. Sullivan's life. Five thirty, before she finally stopped speaking. *Five thirty!* Five forty-five before he was in his car. Six, the rain had started. Six forty, easily, before he was in the shower. Seven, realistically, before he was in front of a warm fire, a shot of bourbon and that great new ITV reality show about the pop band. He checked his watch. It was already ten past six. Fuck it. And everything else.

He was dying for a smoke, too.

He shook his head glumly. It was chucking down various species of pet animals outside, no chance he could open the window even a crack.

'When are they going to put some streetlights on this damn road?' he muttered angrily to himself as he flicked on his brights. 'Pitch fucking black.'

Down the road, only a short distance away, four fourteen-year-old girls jumped off a city bus and clustered together on the side of the carriageway, faces animated, continuing the conversation they'd been having on their twenty-minute ride home from the shopping mall. They were still in their school uniforms – blue skirt, white shirt, blue jumper, blue coat.

The dark had come early that evening, and the four girls blinked as their eyes adjusted to the shadows.

'I hope Adeline and Ollie get picked! They're ah-mazing.'

'And Alicia! Freaking *love* Alicia!'

Around them, the rain was coming down in sheets.

On either side of the road, the bare branches of the trees danced to the howl of the wind.

Despite the weather, the girls were joyful, four happy spirits, all smiles and sweet life.

With clockwork precision, they had returned exactly as planned, just in time for the much-anticipated finale of *Rising Stars*. In exactly an hour, they'd be showered, changed and happily glued to their respective television screens. That night, on live TV, the five judges were going to narrow down the contestants from five to three. This final three would then form their band, the hottest pop trio in the country, their songs almost guaranteed to sweep the charts. Oh, the excitement, the buzz, the seductive thrill of anticipation! The four girls had faithfully promised to call each other the minute the decision was announced.

'Come on, hurry, I don't want to miss the beginning,' the auburn-haired girl said, pulling her coat in a little bit closer.

In twos, they walked down the side of the dual carriageway, away from the bus stop, towards the footbridge that loomed in front of them across the road, half covered in shadows and spook. But this didn't bother any of the girls; this was familiar terrain, home.

'Where's your dad picking you up?' the tall, dark-haired girl asked.

'The usual. Yours?'

'Cool, mine too.'

The other two nodded as well.

To get home, the girls would need to cross the A-road, then walk down to the mouth of the long footbridge that spanned it as well as the busy motorway that ran parallel to it. Up the footbridge, a five-minute walk across both roads, and then down again on the other side would get them to the bottom of the village where they all lived. 'The usual' was here, on the other end of the footbridge, a mutually agreed-upon, tried-and-tested pick-up point that saved the adults the hassle of driving onto and over the usually busy motorway.

'What's so hot about the beginning, then? Do you want another go at ogling at Ricky from last time's recap?' one of the two blonde girls, the buxom one, joked.

'What? No! I just don't like to miss the start, that's all!' the girl with the auburn hair replied, laughing.

'Oh, go on, admit it, you *loooove* Ricky!'

It was true. She did have a bit of a crush on him (didn't every girl in the country?). But she was laughing too hard to reply.

In the distance, there was a flash of lightning followed seconds later by the low growl of thunder. A solitary crow flew straight overhead, then disappeared into the branches behind them, its loud, distinct caws swallowed entirely by the sound of the rain. She was the first to cross. She took a step forward, then stopped and looked left and right. Nothing. All around her seemed eerily deserted, the heavy rain keeping people away, off the roads if they could help it, and in the warm comfort of their homes.

Inside a silver Volkswagen less than ten seconds away, Paul Sullivan was singing along to Eiffel 65's catchy hit, 'Blue'. He was in a slightly better mood; somehow the ironically named song was making things seem that much less so. He sang loudly, turning up the volume with one hand, other hand on the wheel, fingers drumming the beat.

It was right then that he saw the girl. His eyes widened in alarm.

'O Jesus!' he cried, grabbing the wheel with both hands, slamming the brake violently with his foot.

The girl didn't see the car at all.

She was already in the middle of the road when she caught the glare of headlights in her peripheral vision. She had barely turned her head in the direction of the lights when she heard it, that terrific squeal. She screamed.

Paul Sullivan swerved frantically to one side aiming straight for the trees. But inside his head, the synapses were firing, his mind felt electric, not real. Billions of neurons, trillions of connections. He knew. He had seen it. Shrouded in fog. The ghost-child. He had seen it fall. No. More. More than that. *More* than that. He had felt it. He had felt it in his head and in his ears and in the pit of his stomach, that unmistakeable sound, that sickening dull thud.

Within seconds, the car hit the bushes on the side of the road and lurched to a halt, throwing him forward, his chest hitting the top of the wheel, ricocheting back. Somewhere inside, deep, deep inside, he started to feel the first pangs of pain, but he wasn't sure what it was, emanating from the very tips of his toes like that, or even if it was his own pain.

Slowly he opened the door of his car, stumbled out and vomited into the bushes.

There was loud, hysterical screaming – female sounds – coming from somewhere behind the trees, where the road ran straight on. He didn't know who or what the source of the sound was. There was another sound, too, a kind of sharp piercing whistle, persistent, tormenting. It was inside both his ears, inside his head, and it was alive. Wild-like. But he had never heard this sound before and he knew neither what to make of it nor how to rid himself of it.

He sat down, quietly, crouched like an animal, next to a puddle of his own vomit.

He didn't stir. Not even when he heard the sirens or saw the kaleidoscope of flashing lights making a thousand mini suns around him. Or even when they pried apart the bushes and shone the torch directly into his eyes.

Even then, he sat there in the bushes, eyes closed, terrorised, silent and unmoving.

First the sounds fell away, then the lights.

Paul Sullivan felt relief.

The universe turned silent and thick-crayon-black.

Almost

It takes him two hours to tell the story.

Sitting at his kitchen table. Two cups of tea. Ordinary tea. 'Builder's tea', they call it here in England, the name itself betraying all sorts of things, about the tea, about the drinker, about England itself. He hates this name. But yes, 'builder's tea' it's called. It has another name, a more romantic name; it also goes by 'English Breakfast', a name used more commonly by a less common crowd, a crowd that can afford to be sentimental about such things. He doesn't love this second name either. It implies a kind of Englishly polite instruction, as if by virtue of its name alone, it is informing you that its consumption ought to be limited to strictly-before-noon. Even so, it is the only kind he drinks, no matter what the time of day. His father's habit. Builder's tea, you see.

He drinks it with milk. Full fat. Four sugars. Also, his father's habit. It'll kill you one day, they say, this habit of drinking tea with four sugars. 'If you don't want to die young, cut out the sugar,' they warn, the well-meaning experts. But he knows something they don't, a kind of bird's-eye view into this whole dying young business. So, he doesn't go from four to zero or frankly even to three and a half. Wilful neglect of duty. Guilty as charged. Also, his father is still alive. Bless his cold fucking heart.

So.

Sunlight streams in through the windows. It's a glorious July afternoon. Outside, the grassy expanse of Primrose Hill forms a patchwork carpet, undulating swells of green and gold and yellow. Happy flowers make happy multicoloured dots, matching spectacularly the trademark Emma Bridgewater mugs he places on the table.

Somewhere a window is open. You can smell the honeysuckle – fruity, warm, gently erotic. A stray breeze swirls in. There's a buzz. It starts off sporadically, then becomes louder and more constant. It gets punctuated then, a series of dull thwacks. Soon enough, there's a pattern, a sequence, buzz-buzz-thwack-buzz-thwack-buzz-buzz-thwack-buzz-thwack-buzz.

It's ambient. It's starting to become irritating. Also, it is distracting. The thing with the human mind is that it cannot let a sound be a sound, it is compelled to look around for its source, a kind of madness, it will not stop until this happens, until it has found what it is looking for. Breaking concentration, breaking focus. How little it takes to break the mind.

Sure enough his concentration has broken. He wavers. Mid-sentence, he stops speaking. His eyes dart around the room, searching.

There. Found it. Found the culprit. Fly. Fly hitting glass.

He understands this. Glass windows are a recent invention – a pinprick of time in the grand scope of the fly's evolution. It wants to get out. It can't. They have a common provenance in pain, this fly and him, stuck in the space between what is and what could be.

But that's the only sound in the room, this fly buzzing. Poor little stupid trapped thing.

Before the fly, before he wavered, before those things broke, there was the sound of his voice.

Telling the story of a fourteen-year-old girl.

Telling the story of his daughter.

His daughter who died.

PART I: CONVERSATIONS WITH BARTHES

It begins like a children's story.

Once upon a time, there was a family of three

mum
and dad
and daughter.

But then something happened
                          in the middle

that changed the end.

Him

He used to be a professor of poetry. Still is, strictly speaking. But the tension in the tense is the nerve of the story.

For example, he used to be a father. Now he doesn't know what he is. Is he a father or was he a father or did he used to be a father who is no longer a father? Technically speaking, that is. English grammar-wise. He's never needed to think about it in this way, never had to study the morphology of language in this manner with such profound personal relevance.

Nouns also. Proving to be very problematic. Meaning: when you have a common noun that gets its 'identity' from another common noun, and that second noun ceases to exist, does the first noun lose its own meaning, too? Put in a less abstract way, when you have the word 'father' that gets its identity from the word 'daughter', and 'daughter' dies, does 'father' die with it, too?

Ceteris paribus. (Assuming no other complicating factors. Like other children, et cetera.)

You see the problem. He finds it pervasive, infuriating, ever since it all happened, this problem of the tenses particularly, he cannot escape it, it confounds him. *Is/was/used to/lives/lived/died* all take on a new urgency, a new insurgency.

He considers it ironic, to be confounded by language in this way, since he is, after all, a professor of poetry. And what is poetry, but beauty disguised in language. *This* is his job. Language is his job. Also, beauty. Beauty is also his job. Every day, he stands in front of a group of 'the exceptionally bright young people of tomorrow' (whizz kids, wunderkinder, Keatses in the making, every last one), and attempts to discuss the beauty of words, the beauty of beautiful things.

He deals in beauty.

But he is (temporarily) no longer a professor of poetry because suddenly he stopped seeing the beauty of beautiful things.

Which, naturally, posed a problem.

So, he asked to have a sabbatical.

'We understand,' they said at his workplace, 'have a sabbatical! Come back when you're ready! When you are over it! Take your time! Absolute pleasure! Weeks! Months! As long as you need!'

Which would have been generous and kind of them, if not for one little detail:

Broadly speaking, he had forced their hand somewhat, not given them a choice, i.e. he had fucked up. *Specifically* speaking, he had gone back to work ten days after it happened (what was he thinking?) and then had to rush out of one of his lectures (Shakespeare and the iambic pentameter) after spontaneously bursting into tears.

And they had grown alarmed.

This was – just to clarify – before the years when men were patted on the back for crying in public. No. No patting. And no crying, *absolutely* no crying. It was not a thing one did.

So, he had suggested a sabbatical, which was just as well, because if he hadn't, they probably would have anyway.

Can't (they would have discussed in private, shaking their Oxbridge-educated heads gravely) have grown men crying in public like this. Crying while teaching. Crying while teaching

Shakespeare, no less. Simply not. What kind of example would it set for the next generation?

He half agreed.

He'd been badly behaved. Overly emotional, unduly instinctive, unnecessarily soft. Also, utterly self-obsessed to display one's feelings in this manner. Also, unmanly.

So that was the story of his (temporary) (also indefinite) sabbatical.

So, he is/was a professor of poetry.

He also is/was/used to be/still too can be thought of as a bit of a closet theory-head. He especially enjoys the French literary theorists, geniuses one and all.

He decides to open the closet.

He's interested, particularly, in Roland Barthes. For many reasons. Including, but not only because on 25 February 1980, Barthes was fatally hit by a laundry truck when crossing the street in front of the College de France. But it's not just that. It would be most narcissistic of him if it was *just* that. But yes, it's certainly part of the reason, this strange parallel in how they ceased to exist, his daughter and Barthes. Death by vehicular collision. Only Barthes was sixty-four. His daughter was fourteen. Not that he (meaning him) begrudges him (meaning Barthes) those extra fifty years. Or something. Or anything.

But he is filled with a kind of morbid curiosity. The progeny of suicides often are.

He wonders what Barthes has to say about all of this.

Barthes
'Memento illam vixisse.'[1]
(Remember that she lived.)

Him

He is ready to talk about her, his daughter. He is ready in a way. In a way.

Sometimes he talks silently, a kind of muttering, a retreat-into-self; sometimes he speaks out, loud and clear and coherent. Like he *wants* the world to know. He shifts between the two without warning.

He starts with the basics. She was fourteen. She had pale, milky skin just starting to turn teenage-bad on the chin and the cheeks, and thick auburn curls, and deep green eyes, and rather fancied herself (but only privately) to resemble a young Rita Hayworth, whom she had watched in *The Shawshank Redemption* and regarded, irrefutably, as the single reason for Andy Dufresne's freedom.

She lived with her mother and her father (i.e. him) in a modest terraced house on a quiet, tree-lined street in North London by the Heath, a fitting location for a professor of poetry. The Heath! (Keats's Heath! Yes! Shelley's Heath! Byron's Heath! Yes! Yes!) The house she lived in was neither big nor small, neither fancy nor plain. Just middle of the line. Red brick, two-up, two-down. Ordinary. Which word could also be used to describe her professor father, her once-published-since-multiply-rejected novelist mother, her school, her teachers, her friends, her appearance, her clothes, her talents (bar one), her exam results, and broadly speaking her whole life. Nothing was exceptional. Nothing was standout. All of it was ordinary.

One could argue it takes a certain amount of ethical imagination to understand the privilege of the word ordinary. It's not what we are taught to aspire towards; no, it's always the pursuit of the extraordinary that is considered the goal.

But hey ho.

Extraordinary can be superlative, momentous and remarkable (and this is all the pursuing-towards that is expected of us) but it can also be other things. Such as what happened to her. At fourteen. An ordinary girl. An extraordinary thing. With no pursuing required at all.

We rarely get the opportunity to think about this, that's the funny thing, to think about this other side of extraordinary, this side which makes ordinary look so goddamn good. So caught up, the lot of us, in all the pursuing and the hunger and the insatiable demands of being something more than just being. But if we do, if we stop for one blessed second and take it all in, the whole purpose of our existence and everything, we realise what sweet solace it must be to look back upon one's life and think with a great big splash of relief: nothing happened! Nothing extreme, nothing catastrophic, nothing out of the ordinary...

Ever. Happened. To. Me.

Amen.

At fourteen, of course, you can't know this.

Sometimes, not even at sixty-four.

Barthes

'Ignomania...'[2]

Him

He tells the story in two hours.

Two hours.

One hundred and twenty minutes.

Seven thousand two hundred seconds.

Fourteen years of living.

A split-second of dying.

Seven thousand two hundred seconds of trying to condense all that into a story.

Everything gets reduced with time.

Everything.

Milk.

Mountains.

Memory.

Mourning.

Invincibility.

History.

Us.

Barthes

'Don't say mourning. It's too psychoanalytic. I'm not mourning. I'm suffering.'[3]

Him

At his daughter's school once, they asked the kids what they wanted to be when they grew up.

Astronaut, someone said, scientist, doctor, Anna Karenina, race-car driver, tennis player, teacher, Madonna (the singer, it was clarified, not the mother of Jesus), Jesus himself (good students building on previous answers), writer, musician, nurse. One little boy wanted to become a ballet dancer. This, his teachers considered to be an unusual ambition. The parents were called in. Meetings were had. A lot was made of it.

His daughter wanted to become an actress when she grew up. She wanted to dance like Cyd Charisse and sing like Billie

Holiday and rock a black strapless evening dress with long elbow-length gloves, like Audrey. All when she grew up.

Barthes

'Every exploration is an appropriation.'[4]

Him

On the evening it happens, he is waiting in the car. They've planned to do it this way. He will wait in the car, she will come to the car, that's the plan. But then she is late. He frowns. He looks once again at the time, those bright orange numbers on the car's display, numbers made of lines, even the rounded ones like 0 and 2 and 3 and 5 and 6 and 8 and 9, amazing how they can do that with numbers, change their essential shape in that way. Where are these girls? he wonders. It's still pouring. The other cars are also waiting, he recognises the models and makes, he knows them, he knows the people inside them too, though it's raining too hard to see through the windows, to wave or say hello. Once again, he looks at the time. It's not like them to be late. Especially since he knows that TV show is on tonight. His daughter has a disturbing crush on that fellow from Derby. He knows this, too. She may not think he knows, but oh he knows. He knows his daughter, he sees things, how the very top of her cheeks blush when he comes on screen, how her eyes begin to shine when he starts to sing, how until he finishes his song, the Earth stops spinning and everyone else be damned. He has seen all this, and has been taken aback by it, by the adolescent intensity of her passion. He frowns. He doesn't like the fellow from Derby. But, he realises with sudden shock, it's not about him. It's about his daughter's affections. About the idea that she has them at all! For a man.

Other than himself, that is. Gosh, is he jealous? Ridiculous! He's not the jealous type, could never be jealous, not him. No... this is more like a kind of anxiety... a fear or a protectiveness or something else that has no name but is born the instant your child is born, like its invisible twin, troublesome, unyielding, following you around, never going away. That's it. Of course, that's exactly what this is. He doesn't want her to get hurt, that's all. The clock ticks up another orange digit. His engine is running, polluting the planet but giving him heat. Yes, he decides approvingly (of himself) – it's protectiveness. Because that's his job, isn't it, as her father, to protect her from any and all potential harm, whatever shape or colour or gender it happens to come in?

Barthes
'The world (the worldly) is my rival... "You belong to me as well," the world says.'[5]

Him
A silver Volkswagen.
    That is the shape and colour of harm.
    It has no gender. Perhaps, he thinks later, that is just as well.

Barthes
'We know that the war against intelligence is always waged in the name of common sense.'[6]

Him
Something, he cannot put his finger on it – it is vague, amorphous, indefensible to the rationalist – tells him that this is all wrong. He feels it.

He frowns. He has developed crease lines on his forehead, in the gap between his eyebrows. Age, of course. His daughter disagrees. She tells him it is because he frowns too much. He touches that patch of skin now with his index finger. He can feel the lines. He makes himself stop frowning – this takes effort, this kind of deliberate action, a certain concentrated focus – and turns the engine off. Various internal car-parts sporadically begin to click. Hot metal cooling. A ticking object. Ominous, if you think about it in a certain way. He waits for the clicking to stop. Then he looks outside. Against his consent, stubbornly, the frown returns. He braces himself for the wind, pulls the hood of his jacket over his head and gets out of the car.

He is tall, lean, with long legs, a runner's legs. He takes long strides towards the footbridge, climbs up the stairs, walks over the bridge. One quick glance down over the side, and he knows he is right about something being wrong. It's no longer a feeling so much as a (hideous, obscene) confirmation of the feeling.

Below him, there is plenty of commotion, visual and aural, flashing lights, loud noises, a crowd. The gruesome echo of a celebration or a parade.

(*Au contraire*, the Frenchman would remark.)

He begins to run.

From about ten metres away, he can see it, the cause of the commotion. There's a human body on the road, limbs akimbo. He cannot see the face. There's a lot of red. Red hair, the colour of a dying sunset. But also, another red, a different red, nothing natural about this shade of red. Surrounding the body are official-looking people conducting official-looking business. Other people, too, strangers, standing a respectful distance away, looking sad, looking fearful, speaking in shocked, hushed tones. He can't hear what they are saying, but he knows this language.

He deals in language.

There is no beauty in this language, no poetry.

Nobody has noticed him.

'Please, let it not be her,' he says out loud as he starts sprinting towards the crowd.

'Please God, oh God, please, please.'

He has not thought about God in thirty-seven years.

He has not used such language in thirty-seven years.

Barthes
'Is the scene always visual? It can be aural; the frame can be linguistic...'[7]

Him
There falls a grown man. There he falls. A grown man, fallen to the ground, on his knees, legs stretched out, crying like a baby, retching, bent over from the stomach, a perfectly symmetrical upside-down U with a tail. An ancient Egyptian hieroglyphic.

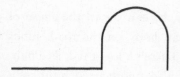

Barthes

'From the terrace of the Flore, I see a woman sitting on the windowsill of the bookstore La Hune; she is holding a glass in one hand, apparently bored; the whole room behind her is filled with men, their backs to me. A cocktail party.'[8]

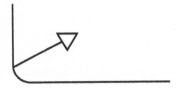

Him

He is still bent over, no shape, no spine. Too heavy for him, the weight of this grief.

He tries to crawl; a baby, an animal.

But he is restrained. Physically stopped from taking another step forward. Encircled by the crowd as if he is not a baby but the other thing, an animal, a wild one, unpredictable in its intentions. To be fair (to the crowd), when he raises his face, his eyes are flaming and he has that exact kind of wild look about him, a thing tormented by some unspeakable terror, a crazed creature. Like a man or a beast with nothing to lose, dangerous, like you don't know *what* he's going to do next.

And therefore, because of that look, that animal look, well-meaning strangers hold him back. He needs to be shielded. Someone has decided that the sight of the dead girl splayed out in the middle of the road will push him over the edge, off the cliff, beyond the pale.

Other people decide such things for you in such situations.

You are reduced, you see, to something incomprehensible.

Barthes

'The world plays at living behind a glass partition; the world is in an aquarium; I see everything close up and yet cut off, made of some other substance; I keep falling outside myself, without dizziness, without blue, into precision.'[9]

Him

'She's not gone yet,' the strangers in the crowd tell him kindly. 'Don't you lose hope. The ambulance is here. Let the doctors do their job. This is their job, you know, to save lives. They are experts in saving lives. You just follow them and don't lose hope. This is the most important thing, remember. Hope. That it mustn't be lost.'

Barthes

'A light without shadow generates an emotion without reserve.'[10]

Him

And now he's got to tell HER (his wife, her mother).

Many years later he will think back to this moment and believe it to be the end of everything.

Barthes

'...something vacant settles in us.'[11]

Him

He has never seen the inside of an ambulance before. He is disconcerted by it, by its particular brand of strangeness.

It has everything a hospital would have. Only, it is compressed, and on wheels. But still, fully stocked. Bed. Drip.

Catheter. Various medical implements. Even an itty-bitty uncomfortable-looking bench for visitors to sit on. Most of all, it has the same smell. Of anaesthetics and death.

Awful places, hospitals, he's always thought, the worst. Even worse than graveyards, because there's no waiting and hoping involved in a graveyard. All that is done away with by then. Not so in hospitals, which is what makes them so alarming. Terrible business, all this waiting and all this hoping. Painful, too (when deep down, you know, you know, you already know).

Yes, he thinks as he scrutinises this one, this mobile hospital, summoned to carry his daughter away, ambulances are just as depressing as hospitals. For sure. It's not like their miniature status diminishes their essential awfulness in any way. They still radiate the same amount of pain.

He's allowed to look at it, inside it, but not to enter it, not to sit on the itty-bitty uncomfortable-looking bench. No, he cannot be allowed to see her, what's left of her.

He knows she will be put on the bed with wheels. More wheels, wheels within wheels. He wonders if she will turn the white sheets red. He knows they're not real sheets, though. Paper sheets, easily disposable. A bed with wheels and disposable sheets. How sinister!

They shut the doors.

The mobile Lilliputian radiator of pain starts to shriek.

He follows in his own car, matching its speed, number for triple-digit number.

Under any other circumstance, this kind of speed would be a thrill.

He throws back his head. Once again, he starts to cry.

Barthes

'The idea that death would be a kind of sleep. But it would be horrible if we had to dream eternally.'[12]

Him

Flashing and shrieking and crying, they arrive at the hospital. Before he can get anywhere near them, they roll her out and roll her away. It is incredible, he thinks, the efficiency of the whole operation. Intricate business, saving lives. Unsure of what he is meant to do, he identifies himself to the plump lady at the front desk who pats him kindly on the arm and asks him to take a seat. *She* knows what he is meant to do. She has been conditioned to know. He is grateful for it. Obediently he finds an empty chair in that big room where there seem to be too many other people exactly like him, scared, waiting.

A little later, when SHE arrives at the hospital, he finds he can hardly believe in anything anymore. It is not what he has feared. It is, if this is possible, worse. SHE is clear-eyed and in control. He doesn't understand HER, this reaction in HER. There's hope, he understands (the kind that mustn't be lost), and then there's blank denial. This second thing is what he sees in HER and it makes him anxious and fearful.

He wants to shake it out of HER physically.

But SHE is impenetrable, untouched by his sadness. Even the way SHE walks in from outside through those double doors, SHE seems oblivious to the darkness, like SHE is floating, like SHE is an angel surrounded by HER own light.

'Where is she?' SHE asks him calmly. 'How long has she been in there?'

Ah, but SHE doesn't know, he thinks, reasoning, rationalising, attempting to eke a bit of sense out of all the nonsense. SHE doesn't know what he knows; SHE hasn't seen what he's seen. And this gives HER a kind of strange power over him.

But he knows that power shifts, so easily, power shifts.

And *this* is what makes him afraid.

Barthes
'Like a kind of melancholy mirage, the other withdraws into infinity and I wear myself out trying to get there.'[13]

Him
How long do they sit there like that, drinking hospital coffee out of paper cups?

Time loses its essence. It becomes both significant and insignificant, equally, and at once.

Fear soars to the ceiling, crashes to the floor, bounces off walls. A kind of madness.

HER parents arrive. For once he is not unhappy to see them. They acknowledge each other formally, nods all around.

'What's the news?' they ask him.

He hates that, the use of that word, how perfunctory it sounds.

But now is not the time.

'No news,' he says quietly.

SHE is still acting perfectly normal. SHE is giving HER parents the details, telling them what happened, how it happened. All with a normal face, in a normal voice. Yes, SHE is calm. SHE is normal. It feels inappropriate, pathological. He has not expected this of HER. How can SHE be calm? How can SHE be normal?

This coffee is terrible, HER mother remarks.

HER father speaks of private doctors and private hospitals. What money can buy; what it can't.

Fear floats upwards like a cloud.

Barthes

'I'm impatient with other people, their will to live, their universe.'[14]

Him

They've been here before, in this place, all four of them together.

Him, HER, HER parents.

On that day his daughter was born.

SHE had been in labour for three days.

HER parents had been outside, waiting, anxious for news (there, that word again); he had been inside, also waiting, but with a different kind of anxiety.

Even then, HER father had advocated for the superior comforts of a private hospital. *He* hadn't been able to afford it. HER father had offered to pay. *SHE* had turned down his generosity. *They* had warred. A colossal row. Post-nuptial disagreement, one could say, in hindsight.

They all sit here now in a mirror image of birth.

Déjà vu.

Barthes

'The art of living has no history: it does not evolve: the pleasure which vanishes, vanishes for good, there is no substitute for it. Other pleasures come, which replace nothing. No progress in pleasures, nothing but mutations.'[15]

Him

Twelve hours pass in a kind of psychedelic puff of terror.

He feels high.

On lack of sleep, on caffeine, on fear. But deep within him is the kind of strange lucidity that makes an addict an addict, allowing you to accept truths you otherwise wouldn't. Or couldn't. Or can't. A kind of mercy. He knows she's gone.

SHE is still holding up impressively well. 'She's going to be okay,' SHE repeats over

and over

and over

and over

and over

and over

and over

and over

and over

and over.

'She's going to be okay.'

But SHE is not high.

Barthes

'Incoherence seems to me preferable to a distorting order.'[16]

Him

At 2pm the following afternoon, after nineteen hours of waiting and hoping, the waiting and hoping ends.

They are called into a room. The door is shut behind them. They are offered water. With bewildered faces, they decline.

Standing before them is a lady doctor. Asian. Very young.

Very beautiful. Big dark eyes. She'd probably be extra beautiful when she smiles. Only, she's not. Smiling, that is.

'I'm really very sorry,' she says simply, 'it was too late.'

He knows this already of course. She's only confirming what he already knows.

And yet, in the face of it, he disintegrates like a made-in-China biscuit or a disturbed dream.

For the second time in twenty-four hours, his body gives. But this time, it actually crumbles like there are no bones, no muscle or tissue or skin, no substance to it, to him, no soul. He slumps into the chair. His neck falls away. His head hits the table. His mouth opens. He lets out a cry. It's a horrible noise. Then the tears come. And they don't stop. This is why, he understands now, this is why everybody is essentially uncomfortable with the idea of a grown man crying. It's just so *ugly*. The tears and the snot and the spit dripping down his face, sticking to facial hair, globules of bodily fluids everywhere. Total unmitigated disaster.

But he cannot help it, this display of ugliness. It's beyond his control. For all his mental preparation in the last nineteen hours, when he hears someone *else* say the words, someone with authority, he feels like his guts have been ripped out, his intestines unwound into a long, very pink snake of human flesh and muscle.

He's so focussed on himself, so selfish in his grief, that at first he doesn't hear it, the shriek that could blow his mind it's so loud, like the ultrasonic shriek from a colony of flying bats. It's HER. HER mouth is wide open, a giant hole – he can see HER tonsils at the very back, two tiny red tongues and they are trembling with this terrific violence – and from this hole

SHE is shrieking, and SHE can't stop. It's a horrible noise. Worse than his horrible noise. In a competition of horrible noises, SHE would win hands down.

(Is it inappropriate to be thinking such thoughts at this time?)

Barthes

'Mad I cannot be, sane I do not deign to be, neurotic I am.'[17]

Him

HER father drops them home.

Nobody speaks.

'Shall we come in?' HER mother asks when they arrive at the house, getting ready to come in (meaning, rhetorical question as usual).

'Not now,' SHE says, 'I'm sorry but please, not now.'

'Oh,' the mother says, mildly surprised by this. But she climbs back into the car and nothing more is said and then they leave.

Inside, SHE sits down on the sofa and begins to cry softly. When he goes to HER, SHE pushes him away. This elicits a kind of intense hurt. But he doesn't hold it against HER. No, he understands. SHE pushes him away, and in turn, he pushes away his hurt. We are the same, and yet we are different; we are each different people. We come alone and we leave alone, and we suffer alone, we become selfish in our suffering. He understands this. He leaves HER alone.

He goes upstairs, he comes back down again. The whole place feels so gone-baby-empty-nest, he doesn't know what to do with himself. He sits down at the kitchen table, a thick slab

of English oak, full of dark knots and streaky honey. He gets
out some paper, a pen. He doodles.

Barthes
'I perform, discreetly, lunatic chores; I am the sole witness of
my lunacy.'[18]

Him
She's gone.
She's dead.
DE-AD
D-E-A-D
D-E
A-D
D
E
A
D
--- (mirror)
D
A
E
D
D-A
E-D
D-A-E-D
DA-ED.
She died.
(This is what he doodles).

Barthes

'I have a disease; I see language.'[19]

Him

Darkness falls.

SHE is still on the sofa in the same position. SHE hasn't stirred. SHE is still crying.

He is still at the kitchen table. He is still doodling.

But then he stands up, opens the back door, goes out into the garden, breathes in the chilly air. Somewhere beyond, blending into their garden, into the melty darkness, is the sprawling expanse (beautiful, wild) of the Heath. (Keats's Heath! Yes. Shelley's Heath! Byron's Heath! Yes! Yes!)

He looks up at the sky; deep midnight blue, still and smoky.

The full moon casts its silver light between two trees. The frost on the grass shimmers. From where he is standing, it makes a pretty picture.

Once, many years ago, when his daughter was very little, he had told her that when people die, they become stars. Not his idea, it is Juliet's. Or rather, Shakespeare's. None of his ideas are his own; everything he knows, he has learned from his texts. Still, it didn't matter, she had loved the idea, his little daughter, when he had told her, she had squealed with girlish delight and asked him to point out her grandmother – his mother – in the sky. After that, sometimes, he would find her in the garden having conversations with her grandmother-star, then she would see him and feel embarrassed and stop. It was an indulgence, they both knew, a bit of madness, but what's wrong with that, he thought then, what's wrong with indulging in a bit of madness once in a while? But – he thinks now, when he looks up at that night sky – but, where are all the stars?

He comes back inside, back to the warmth, back to the kitchen table, back to his pen and paper, back to his doodle. When he was younger, he wanted to be a poet.

Look! Can you see the white ghost of the moon?
Blue branches
Beckoning
Tangled arms
Poking
At pure, soft, velvet
Blackness
Broken
By the crimson glow of Mars
A drop of fire
Burning
Stars, everywhere, silver stars
Sparkling
Sleeping

(Here, he is playing with colours.)

(The last three lines are a fiction.)

(There are no stars. There's too much pollution. He just needed something silver.)

(This is why he can never be a poet.)

Barthes

'Literature is like phosphorus: it shines with its maximum brilliance at the moment when it attempts to die.'[20]

Him

Later – he doesn't know how much later, but at some later time – when he suggests sleep, gently touching HER neck, the bit just below HER hairline where it curves delicately into HER back, where HER skin is bare, exposed, SHE shudders, then looks at him blankly.

'Sleep?' SHE repeats, like SHE does not understand the meaning of the word.

But then, HER face becomes animated.

'Can we freeze her? Do you think we can freeze her until there is more advanced medical technology that can... you know? Bring her back?'

This is what he was afraid of at the hospital.

Jamais vu.

Barthes

'Someone tells me: this kind of love is not viable. But how can you evaluate viability? Why is the viable a Good Thing? Why is it better to last than to burn?'[21]

Him

They used to have a dog that died, a sad-eyed bitch with a weak heart called Tubby.

They'd got her from a litter of spaniels at the shelter just before their daughter was born. The dog had been tiny, a rich-chestnut-coated fluffy thing, even then with a weak heart, but she'd come straight up to HER, licked HER meticulously, not leaving a single dry patch of face. 'That one,' SHE'd said, 'it's got to be that one, I'll take my chances with the heart.'

One day, a few years later, when he was taking her for a walk, Tubby had stopped while crossing the street, sighed quietly and dropped dead, right there bang-smack in the middle of the zebra crossing, neat even in death, her little body fitting precisely in the black space between two white lines. Passers-by opened their own hearts, offered to help, anything at all, just say the word; a little girl in a red-and-white gingham dress started to cry loudly. He had carried the dead dog in his arms all the way home, holding her broken heart as close as he could to his own.

His daughter cried for ten days straight.

Her mother said: 'Don't cry, she's in a better place.'

His daughter replied: 'How can I stop? My sister is dead.'

Barthes

'In the sentence "She's no longer suffering," to what, to whom does "she" refer? What does that present tense mean?'[22]

Him

The next morning, on a whim, SHE decides to go to HER parents for a few days. He doesn't know what's happened through the night to have triggered this idea. SHE'd spent the night on the sofa; he'd spent it in their bed – what could he have possibly done to make HER want to leave? Still, he is encouraging of this suggestion. In an unselfish, considered way, he sees the logic, it is sound – a child needing a parent when they lose a child. A kind of absurd, natural, circular thing. As absurd and natural and circular as a faraway moon holding sway over the seas.

Barthes

'I want to be both pathetic and admirable, I want to be at the same time a child and an adult.'[23]

Him

After SHE leaves, he sleeps.

He dreams that an army of translucent ants has infested the house; they crawl out of drains and toilet bowls, they stream out of taps, narrow cracks in the woodwork, they cover surfaces, they march up and down walls.

He is living amongst the ants. He is living in the ants. He is an ant.

He wakes with a start.

It is not a pleasant dream.

Barthes

'I ask for nothing but to live in my suffering.'[24]

Him

As simple as that, they're both gone and now he is truly alone.

He can't work. Can't sleep. Won't eat.

There is nothing to do, no chores, no tasks, no itemised list of errands that need running.

He cannot remember the last time he had nothing to do.

He doesn't like having nothing to do. It scares him.

And so, on one of those mornings – they are merged together in his mind, those all-alone mornings; all of them can be condensed into one – he tries to enter his daughter's bedroom. He makes it up to the doorway. Then he turns around, goes downstairs, smokes a pack of cigarettes, goes upstairs to his own room and lies sideways on a bed where sleep will not come.

The next morning, he tries again. He stands outside her bedroom. Getting beyond this point requires a certain courage. It is, you see, a unique situation because her bedroom has no door, just the doorframe painted in shiny white. He can take sole credit for this architectural gem. It is a perfectly acceptable doorframe, finished with hinges and everything, only there is nothing to hinge, which means when he gets up to the room, he can see all the way in. He's not ready to see all the way in. This is the thing.

There is a story behind every story. This one, too.

Listen.

About a year ago, his daughter, beautiful and alive, had developed the curious habit of slamming doors. An alternative to discussion (arguing), conversation (yelling), and compromise (swearing), she preferred, they discovered to their euphemistic surprise, to take the higher ground – meaning, say nothing, just slam doors.

He'd been particularly astonished by it, by the fullness of her fury, by how it didn't appear, at least to him, to be 'a phase' with any kind of natural end-point, as well-meaning well-wishers with a wealth of parenting experience had assured them it was, and really by how it never failed, each time it happened, to make his head explode just a little.

Then it happened, as these things happen, as they are bound to happen, sooner or later. The pinnacle and crash of every family drama. It happened one Sunday at lunch. She'd slammed the door four times (to a count) that morning. 'The next time you slam your door,' he said calmly, helping himself to some more roast beef, 'I'm going to take the door off.'

His daughter moved her chair back, stood up, looked him fearlessly in the eye and, leaving her lunch unfinished, went up the stairs to her room and promptly slammed the door.

He closed his eyes.

SHE said, 'You must never issue a threat to a child if you can't follow up on it.'

He sighed, put his fork down. 'What would you like me to do?' he said.

'Go up and take the door off please,' SHE said.

So, he had gone up and taken the door off please.

Which had worked wonders for his head for a short while.

Only some time later, when his daughter swore she would never slam another door in her life if only she could have hers back, and he softened and relented and decided to give her the benefit of the doubt, he couldn't work out how to put the door back on.

That had been a year ago.

So, her bedroom had/has no door.

And now he cannot bear to go into this bedroom-without-a-door.

Barthes
'Justice is always ready to lend you a spare brain in order to condemn you without a second thought.'[25]

Him
I wasn't there

   (This is the part he is fixated upon.)

I wasn't there
I wasn't there
I wasn't there

Barthes
'The grim
egoism (egotism)
of mourning
of suffering'[26]

Him
The thought, the idea, the very suspicion of suspicion that he might in some way be responsible, that some action of his could have placed them all on a happier, parallel path, drives him to a kind of hysteria.

He hurts, all over; all over, he hurts.

Sometimes it is sharp and crushing, other times it comes as a lingering ache, a deep-down-inside soreness. But all the time it lurks, ugly, unyielding, this hurt of his.

His mind wanders involuntarily (but it could be voluntary, too) to other sources of hurt he can compare his own hurt to, a kind of macabre yardstick. It gives him something to think about. He makes a list:

Terrible things that cause terrible hurt
1. heart attack
2. bear attack
3. cracked rib
4. crucifixion
5. unrequited love

6. cramp in your foot in the middle of the night
7. betrayal
8. natural disasters that wipe out entire geographies
9. war
10. broken femur
11. childbirth (never to be self-verified) (thankfully)
12. Irukandji syndrome
13. second-degree burn
14. abscessed tooth
15. kidney stones
16. lingchi
17. stonefish sting
18. penile fracture
19. school shootings and dead children
20. or a single dead child
  (That might happen to be yours.)
  (Well, yes.)

It's what he's spent his entire academic life warning his poetry students about: 'If you're not careful,' (is his warning) 'everything turns into cliché.'

Barthes
'It exists only for me. For you, it would be nothing but an indifferent picture.'[27]

Him
On the fifth day or maybe it is the fourth or the eighth, he tries once again to enter the bedroom-without-a-door.

And feeling something, not sadness, not pain, something else, something more potent, something too intricate, too evolved to even attempt to find for it some kind of language, he steps inside.

But it knocks him down, this feeling-without-language, the minute he steps into the bedroom-without-a-door. It *physically* knocks him down like a kind of invisible force and he finds himself losing balance, toppling sideways, reaching his arm out to steady himself, and finding nothing to grasp, no seabed to anchor his sadness into, he finds himself sitting in the middle of her bed. The bed she used to lie in. Eyes heavy with sleep; butterfly kisses and goodnight Daddy. And now he is crying. And now he is comforting himself by holding her pillow like it is a live thing with a beating heart, like it's her, but it is not her, of course, only it seems like it is her because it has (a list):

1. her smell
2. three strands of red hair
3. a water-marked spot of dried-out dribble

Barthes
'What I hide by my language, my body utters.'[28]

Him
He makes another list. List-making, he thinks, *may* just be the antidote to grief. Maybe he can cure his grief this way. Maybe there is no other cure, maybe you just go through life making lists. It should be prescribed, he thinks. Handed over to grieving people in an official document, preferably blue, signed by a qualified grief-doctor.

'Feeling sad?'
'Make lists!'
'Feeling mournful?'

'Make lists!'

'Feeling hopeless?'

'Make lists!'

(Medically approved and certified.)

(With guaranteed results.)

(Quack. Quack. Quack.)

So, he makes his list. Properly this time, a formal list, a serious list to be taken seriously. Doctor's orders. He makes it on paper, by hand, using a ruler, drawing rows and columns, concentrating on the straightness of his lines, the shape of his alphabets. It's important to him, the straightness of his lines, the shape of his alphabets.

This list is called Keep v. Give Away. Meaning her belongings from her room. Meaning what used to be her belongings from what used to be her room. Keep v. Give Away. Very original. And practical. And grief-curing.

Keep	Give Away
All photographs	Clothes, shoes etc. Or Personal effects (formal term for formal list)
Old birthday cards	Multiple posters of unknown men

Books	Maths test hidden under bed (47%) (poor result by dead student) (but what kind of punishment does that deserve?)
Pink ballet tutu	Breast enhancing cream
Pillow with her smell	Everything else
	I miss you
	I miss you
	I miss you
	I miss you
	Miss
	Missing
	Missing
	SHIT

Barthes

'The imperfect is the tense of fascination: it seems to be alive and yet it doesn't move: imperfect presence, imperfect death; neither oblivion nor resurrection; simply the exhausting lure of memory.'[29]

Him

Sometimes, when she was very, very young, like four or five or six, and came up to his waist at full height and had tiny little hands and tiny little feet, he would tuck her into bed under the duvet and SHE would read her stories. SHE did the different voices and everything, and *she*, their tiny little red-haired replica-of-her-mother (with nothing of him at all) (except perhaps the particular angle of her left cheek) would giggle and giggle and giggle and then suddenly before the last giggle was over, it would metamorphose into an enormous yawn – so big for someone so little – and before *that* was fully complete, she'd be fast, fast asleep, and her breathing would become soft and rhythmic, a little baby beat to which her little baby chest danced, rising and falling, rising and falling. And they would be amazed by how quickly that all had happened, and they would look at each other and then look at her and think how she was the cutest little thing in the whole wide world and what a miracle it was that she was made out of them. Well, mainly out of HER.

This memory causes him severe abdominal pain.

Barthes
'Regretted: Imagining himself dead, the amorous subject sees the loved being's life continue as if nothing had happened.'[30]

Him
SHE rings to say SHE won't be coming back until after the funeral.

SHE can't face being home, SHE says, without their daughter, the place is empty, it has no meaning.

'No problem,' he says, 'you do that. You take your time.'

Barthes
'Language is never innocent.'[31]

Him
He remembers an essay he'd written once in his own college days. It seems a lifetime ago, but it comes back to him now. It

had been a sad, strange topic, but then his professor had been a sad, strange man.

He wonders what adjectives his own students privately use to describe him. Intellectual, they might say, intense, funny (he hopes), interesting (sometimes), aloof, serious... (self-serious)?

He'd been serious as a student, certainly – very serious, very earnest, studious. He'd wanted to please, in particular, the professor, the sad, strange one, with his permanent stubble and his coffee breath, and his brilliant, austere, theoretician's mind, thinking him sad, thinking him strange, while all the time secretly wishing his own father was more like him, wishing he could talk to his father like he talked to this professor, about Dickens and Foucault, just casually, like a discussion of the day's weather, across the kitchen table, over tea and toast.

In any case, as a serious student, he had taken the essay (the sad, strange one) seriously.

'The saddest word.' (This was the topic.)

He thinks of it now, of the hours and days he had spent poring over books, thinking about the topic, trying to answer the question (for it was a question, really, a big and difficult question disguised as a fragment, that much he knew). There had been a lot of debate over it in the books he had pored over – the question was a philosophical one inasmuch as it was a literary one, and many philosophical questions are not designed to have answers, he learned this too, or answers with any kind of final objective truth (all philosophical answers, however, he believed were questionable), but he found an answer he could live with and he settled, perhaps not very originally, but finally, on 'almost'.

This done, he had proceeded to write a 3,000-word essay on that single word, 'almost'. *Almost won, almost done, almost normal, almost there, almost fair.* And so on. Could have, should have, would have, didn't. So close, so far, the thing that never happened; what could be sadder than 'almost'? 3,000 words, then. 3,000 words that had earned him the precious praise of his alternate-universe father. 'Almost good enough to be published,' the professor quipped when handing him his paper back.

How was I so smart then? he thinks wistfully now. Where has all that gone?

He sees this in his students. Brilliant minds, naturally creative impulses, well-formulated ideas, remarkable capacity for argument, the makings of a whole generation of geniuses. We are at our cleverest at a certain age, he thinks. Fearless, too.

'This is who I am,' (we say at that bold, brave age). 'And this is what I can do.'

Then it all seems to dissipate very quickly, all the cleverness, all the courage.

And all you are left behind with is nothing.

Nothing. Which just might, he thinks now with the benefit of hindsight, be the saddest word of all.

(Well, almost).

Barthes

'There is an age at which we teach what we know. Then comes another age at which we teach what we do not know; this is called research. Now perhaps comes the age of another experience: that of unlearning, of yielding to the unforeseeable change which forgetting imposes on the sedimentation of the knowledges, cultures, and beliefs we have traversed.'[32]

Him

A week goes by.

Already!

It is time for his daughter's funeral. His daughter's funeral!

He has always been particularly mortified when it comes to funerals. Dismal rituals, he has always thought, serving no practicable purpose but to force:

a) The dead to die again, only this time in public.

b) The living to re-live the whole of their grief.

And yes, to think of death, to talk of death, to accept, yes – to *accept* death.

But he cannot. He will not. How can he? How can anyone?

Later on, he will admit openly and without hesitation that he can't remember very much of what happened at his daughter's funeral. 'It was all a bit of madness,' he will say and change the subject.

It is not entirely untrue, for on the day, he is dazed, ineffectual, incapable of action or emotion. No feeling, more dead than the dead. It seems the only way.

He is surprised at the number of people gathered there in the small church, half the village, the whole school, everyone a stranger. Unknown hands shake his, eyes cry, mouths open, speak words he cannot comprehend. But who the fuck are you?

SHE is there, of course, with HER parents. They hug. Like old friends. There's no room for intimacy here. No, intimacy needs to breathe. Else it stifles and suffocates. On the day of his daughter's funeral, there is no room. For intimacy to breathe.

The church is HERS, it has served HER family for five generations, and whatever his personal problems with HER father might be, to the man's credit, his propitious coming into wealth hasn't propelled him to shift his patronage to fancier quarters.

And so it stands, a simple stone structure, unpretentious, unpretty, on uneven cobbled stone, flanked by a pair of silver birches that in another month would proffer a semi-circular canopy of happy bright green to the whole construction. Now, the branches are bare, offering no embellishment, no colour, no cheer.

Inside, it is as basic as it is on the outside; wooden beams run across the vaulted ceiling, wooden pews sit on the stone floor, narrow panels of stained glass along the side walls fling in a modest splash of colour. The only truly beautiful feature is on the back wall, a rather elaborate oil painting framed in ornately carved dark oak, depicting the crucifixion of Christ.

As the father of the dead person, he has a front row seat, a cause for celebration on any other occasion, in any other venue. He takes his seat, unspeaking, stunned. He is cold, he realises suddenly, although outside it is bright, uncommonly warm for this time of year. The sun makes the stained glass look pretty, producing miniature rainbows that dance along the walls and on the floor with a kind of misplaced gaiety.

Dozens of people file in. Organ music is already playing. On his seat is a hymn book and a funeral programme. SHE has organised it all; he couldn't bear to be involved.

The rest is a blur; what he remembers is random.

Fragments of a father's discourse.

The heavy double doors swing open; his daughter enters in a box carried by eight boys from her school, kids with beautiful, innocent faces who haven't lived long enough to touch death. And yet here they are, in two neat lines of four, carrying it in.

The organ music stops. Whitney Houston takes over. *I will always love you*, she swears.

Then it is quiet. Somewhere a muffled cry, a cough, the rustle of pages turning in perfect sync.

The priest clears his throat. He says something. He stops. People sing. They stop singing. The priest says something else. He stops. People sing. They stop singing. This happens three or four times. Then SHE speaks. SHE speaks beautifully, movingly, about her, their daughter. SHE speaks with tenderness and love. He marvels at HER, marvels at the somethingness inside HER that has fled in fear from inside him.

SHE stops speaking then, sits down. There is a moment when all around him is silent, except it's not – the whole church is crying! This, he thinks, must be what it sounds like. When the world cries. This is as close as he will ever get to experiencing it.

Then it's over.

The doors swing open again; his daughter exits in a box carried by the same eight boys with the beautiful faces, only their innocence has been altered now, permanently and forever more.

He follows its departure with his eyes.

Whitney is back on, singing up a storm.

Saying goodbye, asking him not to cry.

Barthes
'Miseries of a birth.'[33]

Him

He finds he has a bit of clarity. He knows what he wants.

He wants to walk barefoot on the burning sands of an imaginary desert until he can walk no more, he wants to fall on his knees and scald the skin on his legs until it blisters and foams, he wants to look up at the scorching sun until it blinds him and takes away his vision, he wants to scream from his parched throat, until the sound makes him deaf.

Take me, take me, take me.

Just take me instead.

Barthes

'Idea of suicide; idea of separation; idea of withdrawal; idea of travel; idea of sacrifice, etc.'[34]

Him

Bad ideas.

Barthes

'Anxiety mounts; I observe its progress, like Socrates chatting (as I am reading) and feeling the cold of the hemlock rising in his body; I hear it identify itself moving up, like an inexorable figure, against the background of the things that are here.'[35]

Him

At the burial, somebody touches his arm. He looks up to see an old lady he doesn't recognise. She is tall and thin; black clothes and white hair. She is dabbing her dry eyes with a wet handkerchief.

'Don't worry,' she says, 'it will get better with time.'

'No,' says a man on his other side, whose only son had once driven into a tree and died. This man he recognises, but cannot at this moment name. He is a colleague at the college. A professor of ethics and moral philosophy. He has a small moustache and a big nose. If the terrible thing had not happened, the boy, his son, would have been forty-two. At the time of driving into the tree he had been twenty-two. Which made, if not for anything else, then for easy maths. 'No,' the man repeats definitively, with (exactly) two decades of intimate experience under his belt. 'It will not get better with time.'

He doesn't understand what they say, cannot, he cannot grasp their meaning at all. Neither of them makes any sense to him. Not the woman he doesn't recognise, nor the man he does.

Before him, a scene unfolds. It is dramatic and very, very sad. They are lowering the casket. Nothing more needs to be said. They are lowering the casket. That's all.

He averts his eyes. Slowly, bit by bit, she goes in; slowly, bit by bit, they come out... feelings. Like a drip into the vein – unnatural, foreign, familiar, vital – feelings return. Sadness, sudden and desperate. Pain, sharp, from somewhere in his stomach. Or it could be his chest. And something else – if he allows it – guilt. Shockingly powerful waves of guilt that terrify him... he knows they could submerge him if he isn't careful, carry him away. And arising from the waves, another emotion – a dangerous one – anger, which seeps in, metallic and molten like coagulated blood, bursting out of that drip-fed vein, taking control of his senses, taking him by surprise. It is a terrible anger. But directed at what? At life? At God? At those waves of guilt that tease and torment? But also, perhaps, at other things.

At everything, at everyone. At the cemetery, at her grave, at the strangers that surround it, at his wife and HER parents and his own father who is stooped over and who cannot stop crying, and even, but just only for a flash, at his dead daughter – how could you be so irresponsible? How could you die? How could you make me go through this? But, he is surprised by this, by his own anger. He is not an angry man.

He tries to block the feelings, focus on his duties and responsibilities instead. Duties and responsibilities. Yes. He goes about them with machine-like precision, in the manner of a father with a dead daughter. As behoves such a person. Behoves. What a word!

He doesn't attend the wake. He has no interest in attending the wake. He will deal with HER wrath later, which will come, inevitably, regarding the matter of his being selfish and irresponsible (and an embarrassment) (and also a horror). 'You outdid yourself today,' SHE will say, 'no mean feat, that. I mean, what were you *thinking*? This was your *daughter's* funeral! You disappeared at your own daughter's funeral? Just disappeared! For once in your life, just *once*, you could have made it not about you. But, no, you couldn't help yourself, not even this once!'

But all that will come later. And he will be ready for it. But for now, he just needs to leave. He simply cannot bear to be there with all those people. And so, he leaves. He disappears. At his own daughter's funeral. Yes.

No one notices the broken-hearted man as he separates himself from the crowd, slips out of the house, through the garden door. He walks back alone to the church yard, crouches quietly by his daughter's grave.

The sun has shifted. It is silent. This is solitude.

He touches the tombstone; it feels smooth, cool. With his index finger he traces the etched letters of his daughter's name. He speaks it out loud. For the first time that day, he allows himself to cry.

It is on this day then, in this last moment, when the salty tears start from his eyes, and run down the contours of his face, down his neck, down into the earth, collecting in a small foamy pool by his feet, watering his daughter's grave, seeding his own sadness, that something strange happens.

The setting sun spreads its burnished light over the sea of tombstones, and in this place of death and decay, everything turns momentarily alive with floating stripes of orange and gold.

Goodbye, my little girl, he whispers, goodbye.

And it is then, in this precise moment, that their roles reverse.

He regains control. SHE loses it.

Barthes
'Each of us has his own rhythm of suffering.'[36]

PART II: THE RHYTHM OF SUFFERING

Him

He is looking for a very specific poem.

'This Be The Verse' by Philip Larkin.

(Google it.)

He's taught this poem before.

Every English professor in the country worth his salt has taught this poem before.

It's one of those poems, and Larkin is one of those poets.

Also, his mother used to read Larkin.

(Go on. Google it.)

He reads it now. Then he reads it again.

He agrees with Larkin:

Every family is a kind of political set-up.

It starts off as a dictatorship. Joint dictators, mum and dad, sharing power, sometimes badly. Exhibiting strange behaviours. Not exactly embodiments of kindness and virtue. Not – most times – the benevolent gods they claim to be.

They make the rules for everyone else. What to do, when to do it, how to do it, why. Tyranny, really. Yes, they are dictators; they hold the power. And so, they dictate; they exhibit that power.

The universe breathes silently. Little people grow up. Things shift. They are subtle, these shifts, imperceptible, tiny shifts of time, of position, of power.

Experimentation begins.

Pushback. Murmurs. The stirrings of civil unrest.

'Can I say no?' the little people start to wonder.

'No...' At first, it's only a whisper, pliable, tentative... 'No.'

(Gasp) 'I can say no! I've just said no!'

It gets bolder, louder, more confident. 'No!'

'No! No! NO!'

The fault lines crack. The dictatorship begins to weaken.

A few more years pass.

It's overt now. The shift in power. You see it.

Continental drift: Landmasses split over time, minute, undetectable shifts. And then you see them. After the fact. Wondering how something so big could have happened like that, so quietly, in front of your eyes and under your nose.

No. *No!* I'm *not* going to do that. You have no right. I will not live under this oppression.

Tears. Raised voices. Or simply slamming doors.

Hurt. Confusion. Betrayal. Love.

Gratitude. Ingratitude.

Cake! Cake! Let them have cake.

Understanding. Misunderstanding.

You don't have a clue, you pathetic people!

Overrule. Overthrow. Off with their heads.

It is a revolution.

Then: Exhaustion. War is tiring. Peace is easier. Come in a bit, you come in a bit. Let's meet in the middle.

Negotiation. Compromise. Truce.

The seeds of democracy are slowly sown. It grows, it blooms. It flourishes.

Order. Finally, some order in our newly established democratic family! Long may it prevail!

She dies.

Anarchy sets in.

Barthes

'What relation can I have with a system of power if I am neither its slave nor its accomplice nor its witness?'[37]

Him

Her mother, his wife, sits on the sofa all day, surrounded by visitors.

So many visitors. All the time. Constantly, they are constantly there. It's been over a month, but they won't stop coming. They come for HER. He's made it clear he would prefer not to have any company.

This hasn't gone down well. Not with the visitors. Nor with HER.

'Ungrateful,' SHE says to him once, 'why must you always be so ungrateful?'

Then he feels a little bit of guilt. But only a little. He'd still rather they all went back to their own homes, he'd be grateful for that.

'It's not like they're doing it for themselves,' SHE says, 'they're doing it for *us*.'

SHE explains this distinction like it matters.

He doesn't even know who half of them are, he's never seen them before, none of them ever bothered to show up when his daughter was alive. They're all exactly the same, he notices, these visitors, their gestures, their behaviours, even the body language, the shaking of heads, proffering of hugs, blowing of noses – like they've all attended some kind of class; like they've all been expertly schooled in grief.

To these people, he realises, he is no longer himself, nor SHE HERself – no, they are no more him or HER, or even him-and-HER, but a brand-new identity, which is a collective identity, which is a parents-of-a-dead-child identity. (What, he wonders as an aside, do you even call parents-of-a-dead-child, other than parents-of-a-dead-child? There are widows and widowers and orphans but no word, nothing at all, to define their existing state(lessness).) And so, these visitors *need* them, the new two of them, the parents-of-a-dead-child them, to be very, very sad and very, very stricken all the time. Yes, it seems to him that this state of being is necessary on behalf of everyone else, because now they are significant in some deeper way in the wider world, as parents-of-a-dead-child, they are symbolic, they represent by their very existence the greatest possible loss of all.

This fascinates him. It fascinates him greatly, in a thought-provoking, academic kind of way.

(SUBJECT: GRIEF

CLASS: ANTHROPOLOGY

DEPARTMENT OF FUCKING HUMANITIES.)

But this is the only thing that fascinates him.

Other things are less thrilling. Such as the odd compulsion these people have to bring things. Strange things, too. Blankets. Teabags. Candles. Food. The house is full of donated food. Fish pie. Roast chicken. Soup. Macaroni and congealed cheese. Cake. Lots of cake. All shapes and sizes and flavours of cake. And wine, all colours and ages of wine, bottles and bottles of wine.

Her mother, his wife, doesn't seem to care much for the food; mostly it gets thrown away. But SHE seems to have developed an affinity for the wine. Yes, SHE seems to like the wine a lot. And the blankets and the candles. Also, the visitors. SHE likes the visitors. The ones who are constantly there, everywhere he looks; they fill the house with their presence, like rats. Sometimes he thinks he prefers rats.

But SHE likes them, the visitors. So, SHE sits on the sofa in their little sitting room that SHE lights with the new candles, and SHE covers her shapely legs with a new blanket, and SHE drinks the new wine. Surrounded, the whole time, by the scurrying visitors.

SHE exists in their halo.

When they leave, SHE seems to fade away.

In s-l-o-w-m-o-t-i-o-n.

Like London mist.

Barthes

'Everyone is "extremely nice" – and yet I feel entirely alone. ("Abandonitis").'[38]

Him

Sometimes, it is not what's said that haunts you.

It's what's left unsaid.

'Why weren't you at the bus stop?' SHE has *not* asked.

Barthes

'I am interested in language because it wounds or seduces me.'[39]

Him

Loss... (he doodles)
Grows inside you
An extra appendage, a fluttering wing

A voice inside your head
'Hello. I'm here to stay!'
Forever; forever more.
Physical. A thingamabob. A whatchamacallit. An object.
Sharp. Heavy. Enormous in size.
The shape and colour of Poe's Raven's eyes.
Nevermore!

'God,' he writes at the bottom of the page, 'that was truly terrible.'

Barthes

'To try to write love is to confront the muck of language: that region of hysteria where language is both too much and too little, excessive and impoverished.'[40]

Him

He smokes.

He's always smoked.

His mother smoked.

His father never smoked. Told his mother never to smoke. Told him never to smoke. That's why he smokes. That's why he's always smoked.

But now he smokes more than he's always smoked. He smokes a pack in one sitting. Or three. Or four.

He smokes them back-to-back, sitting in his armchair in a room lit only by the blue glow of the plugged-in computer and the cigarette itself, the circular orange fire of its burning tip.

'It'll kill you,' SHE warns.

He finds that oddly funny. He laughs.

'Fuck you,' SHE says, and he knows he deserves that.

Barthes

'God exists, the Mother is present, but they no longer love.'[41]

Him

He and his own father are on shaky ground.

They haven't spoken – as in really spoken, meaningfully spoken – in years, since long before his daughter was born, long before he got married.

He cannot trace it back, though he's tried many times, to exactly when the breaks began to appear. Sometimes he thinks they were always there, just invisible, just beneath the surface until the point they were no longer invisible, no longer beneath the surface. He thinks of them as breaks or cracks rather than chasms or holes because they are not obvious, not openly visible, *never* discussed. No, they are Englishmen and the cracks between them are English cracks, fine and subtle and sophisticated, existing without drawing attention to their existence, but breathing, growing, silently, insidiously until they grow wide enough for one of them, if they don't watch out – little trip, small misstep – to fall headlong into.

The first real confrontation, if you could call it that, occurred when he received the letter from *that* university. A builder's son! A northerner at that! Accepted by *that* university, invited to be *a part of that* university. The contents of the letter, when it had been shared, had been met – he still remembers vividly – not with joy or pride or even, at the other end of the spectrum, with anger or resentment, but with that particular variety of bewilderment that no one, not him nor his father, knew quite how to handle. *That* university wanted someone like him? And for free?

When the bewilderment had faded, his father had advised him not to go. He had gone.

His choice of subject had led to more bewilderment.

(*Imagine that*, his father had offered in his own letter back, after he'd written to say he'd decided what he wanted to study. *A son of mine, a POET! Imagine that! Our very own William Shakespeer. WILLIAM SHAKESPEER! Your mum and I are proud of you, we are. But don't you become Poncy now, son,* he had concluded, *don't you forget where you come from! Don't you forget to write to us.*)

This is the thing no one tells you about moving forward, upward. No one talks about the things you have to leave behind.

His mother's death six years earlier had not helped matters much.

Nor how she died.

Nor how creepy it was that his father still spoke of her in the present tense.

Nor, eventually, had his own choice (or class) (meaning middle, meaning cabbage, meaning chips) of bride.

At some point much later in life it came to him, like a kind of revelation, that it was all connected, of course, all of it, all those seemingly unrelated events from his earliest childhood – the subtle insults, the silent indignities, the tiny aggressions, the imperceptible gestures of resistance – all interlinked, all conspiring together, part of an elaborate plan in which the strings were being pulled by some unknowable outside force, but of which he was the sole protagonist. Eventually he came to make sense of this, to discern that the purpose of everything that had happened to him, the whole point of his life thus far, was to embolden him to reject the very thing his father had, for his entire life, tried so hard to preserve.

The minute he had understood this had been the minute he found the courage to cut it, that frayed and damaged rope that still held them together for no good reason beyond biology and chance. And so, he had cut the rope and walked away, feeling freedom, feeling relief for the first time in his life, not feeling like he had to watch for those fissures anymore, those dark, dreary, working-class cracks that could make him lose his footing at any point and stumble and fall. Fall into that underground cell he often dreamed about, which terrorised him in those dreams, that prison with no ladder with which to climb up and crawl out of the skylight above, because of course there was no skylight either, nowhere to go, no way up, no way out. Just him and his father with his builder's tools (sharp, dangerous) standing in a dark corner, the older man laughing; laughing at him.

Kafkaesque.

But then SHE never understood this, how one could sever ties like this, how one could walk away from one's own blood and not be consumed in guilt. So, SHE had tried. To HER credit, SHE had tried. After they were married, for many years, SHE had tried to mend the bridges between father and son, first just after they had been married and then again, with renewed vigour, when their daughter had been born. In both instances, nothing had come out of it. But then, how could SHE have known that pride and shame, ancient emotions both, existed for this father-son duo on the same continuum; that one man's pride was the other man's shame. So SHE had tried and SHE had failed, because how far can you get, even with the best of intentions, how far can you get when all you have to work with, your only useful tool in the box, is a yellowing photograph of a smiling dead woman with extraordinarily blue eyes, who provided for these two men, blinded by all their pride and all their shame, their only true understanding of love.

Barthes

'A paradox: the same century invented History and Photography...'[42]

Him

The walls feel like they are closing in. He can't bear being in the house anymore, filled with all these people, all the time.

He starts to think of them as less like rats who (albeit with some active intervention) get poisoned or run away, and more like bathroom fixtures, or like grief, part of the house, there to stay.

It's been two months and he hasn't had a single opportunity to speak to HER alone.

Barthes

'The bastard form of mass culture is humiliated repetition... always new books, new programs, new films, news items, but always the same meaning.'[43]

Him

Beyond the visitors that haunt the house, there are the ghosts.

Wherever he looks, they are there, the ghosts of his dead daughter, he can't escape them.

Every wall, every surface, is sprinkled with her presence.

Watching him.

Evaluating him.

Observing how he deals with this new life without her.

If this was a test, he would fail it spectacularly.

His performance has not been impressive.

He has not yet learned the texture of grief.

Barthes

'To see someone who does not see is the best way to be intensely aware of what he does not see.'[44]

Him

SHE appears before him like an apparition.

SHE has a bottle of wine in one hand, an empty glass in another. This is when SHE's trying to work out the point of the glass when the bottle will do.

'You really are some goddamn piece of work,' SHE proclaims. 'What kind of shite throws away their dead daughter's stuff without checking with the dead daughter's mother?'

SHE is very drunk.

'Please,' he says placatingly, 'someone had to do it and I thought it would be too painful for you.'

SHE laughs. Not a laugh-laugh. Meaning a happy laugh. This laugh he believes to be more of a 'go-fuck-yourself' laugh.

SHE narrows HER eyes. SHE says: 'You thought? You *thought*? No, Professor. You didn't think at all.'

Somewhere in the fog of his mind, he hears the sound of a doorbell.

'Go fuck yourself,' SHE says, almost spitting out the words.

Then off SHE goes to answer the door because more visitors with trays full of macaroni and cheese have arrived.

At least, he thinks, he can still interpret the various shades of his wife's laughter.

Barthes

'Mourning. At the death of the loved being, acute phase of narcissism: one emerges from sickness, from servitude. Then, gradually, freedom takes on a leaden hue, desolation settles in, narcissism gives way to a sad egoism, an absence of generosity.'[45]

Him

Then there was another thing that happened.

There was the inquest of the driver of the silver Volkswagen. It would be the first and last time the two men would meet. The man was only young, but his eyes looked old. Yellow, decaying, afflicted by some terrible pain.

What no one knew, could never know, was that the man's eyes reflected a strangeness in his flesh, for if he took off his shoes and peeled back his socks, you would see the toes of his right foot, crooked and misshapen and frozen in that same pain, the foot he had used to slam on the brakes, an old man's foot in a young man's skin, the foot that couldn't save a fourteen-year-old girl, the foot that had failed him when it mattered most. His other foot was young and supple, untouched by the strange condition of its other half for which the best foot doctors in London had no name.

'You must hate him,' people said, 'you must wish him dead. Or at the very least locked up for the rest of his life.'

An eye for an eye. Hammurabi's code. But you see, he knew it wasn't that simple. It is never that simple. Even Hammurabi's code, he knew was not that simple.

In his own grief-stricken eyes, the other man had committed no crime. He hadn't been drinking, he hadn't been speeding, he hadn't been driving on the wrong side of the road like a learner or an American. Only that by some unexplained force of the universe that conspires to make certain things happen how they happen, the man had been there, his daughter had been there, two people destined never to meet. It happens in the opposite way with love. This also, was like that, like love, an accident of space and time, only the wrong way round.

So, he didn't want the man dead or locked up. He didn't believe in retribution of that kind.

On that day, in that courthouse, in that room where judgment is wielded by men on men, he remembers looking into the eyes of the man who had accidentally killed his daughter and seeing only a terrible anguish.

He walked up to the man with the crooked toes and the terrible eyes and put his hand on his shoulder. 'Wrong place, wrong time,' he said, liberating him with more cliché.

THE CODE OF HAMMURABI: LAW #196

If a man has destroyed the eye of a man of the gentleman class, they shall destroy his eye...

If he has destroyed the eye of a commoner... he shall pay one mina of silver.

If he has destroyed the eye of a gentleman's slave... he shall pay half the slave's price.

(His specific situation, you see, is not exactly covered.)

Barthes

'One day, quite some time ago, I happened on a photograph of Napoleon's youngest brother, Jerome, taken in 1852. And I realized then, with an amazement I have not been able to lessen since: "I am looking at eyes that looked at the Emperor." Sometimes I would mention this amazement, but since no one seemed to share it, nor even to understand it (life consists of these little touches of solitude), I forgot about it.'[46]

Him

Then, there's this whole thing with work.

In an act of what can only be labelled 'major misjudgement by momentary madness', he does that stupid thing, he goes back to work.

Too soon, of course. The absolute intersection of foolishness and hubris.

But on the day, at the time he is doing it, it doesn't feel too soon. It feels strangely like freedom.

On the bus, on his way to work, he sits on the very front seat of the top deck (his dead daughter used to love sitting on those seats) and thinks of how in 1941 Miss Phyllis Thompson became licensed as a wartime double-decker bus driver, the first woman in the UK to drive the double-decker bus. He doesn't know why he thinks about Miss Phyllis Thompson. Or why he even knows this touching but totally useless piece of trivia. Or how it's relevant to anything at all. Maybe it is because she is courageous, this Miss Phyllis Thompson, in a way he doesn't feel about himself with any kind of conviction.

He thinks about his own job. About how, for all practical purposes, it serves no purpose at all. How ridiculous it is that he gets paid for talking about other people's pretty words. (His father of course would concur.) His best friend from uni, Jojo Afenynu, is a paediatric surgeon in Liverpool and works night shifts in A&E. *He* resurrects dead poets. Jojo resurrects dying children. They both get called 'Doctor'. Life, he thinks, is not fair.

At his own place of work, they are both surprised and a little bit shocked to see him back so soon. There's some awkwardness as he enters the English and Modern Languages staff room. People abandon dipping teabags in hot water. They shift uncomfortably from one foot to another. The men straighten their ties. The women tuck stray curls behind their ears. Nobody knows what to say. So many different tongues in that little room and nobody knows what to say.

He thinks of Jojo Afenynu. He thinks of Phyllis Thompson. He feels bold and brave. He boils himself some water, dipping his teabag until the thing is strong and potent, a very rich, very dark brown. Totally caffeinated, mildly intoxicating. He reads his lecture notes. He feels ready. But then he goes and ruins everything by crying in the middle of a lecture. Renegade tears with no sense of place. Very bourgeois pantomime.

They are not impressed.

They think he is operating with unsound mind, a mind unhinged by loss.

They are not exactly wrong, he has to admit. It is a strange sight to see a grown man cry. Strange and distressing. Also, unnerving. And in the middle of a Shakespeare lecture at that. Shakespeare! So full of beauty. But Shakespeare! Also, so full of death.

'How do I love thee?' thought Elizabeth Barrett Browning in 1850. 'Let me count the ways.'

'How do I kill thee?' thought Shakespeare some two hundred years earlier. 'Let *me* count the ways.'

A list then. Certainly, he feels, this demands a list.

Death in Shakespeare, a comprehensive list:
1. Drowning
2. Beheading
3. Stabbing
4. Poisoning
5. Also, stabbing then poisoning
6. Snakebite
7. Hanging
8. Dismemberment then fire
9. Blinding of eyes
10. Ripping apart by mobs
11. Starvation
12. Indigestion
13. Cannibalism
14. Consumption of hot coals
15. Consumption by bears

Also,
16. Death by shame
17. By shock
18. By grief

by grief

by grief

by grief

They tell him to go away and come back when he is ready.

The specifics of what that means and when that will be are not discussed. This, he views as a kind of kindness.

Barthes
'Death liberated from dying.'[47]

Him
At home, he is still pottering around with nothing to do. He decides to cook breakfast. Fried eggs and bacon burnt to a crisp, just the way his daughter liked. His wife, too. The two would fight over the bacon and he would smile. Girls will be girls. This was before.

Before. Before. When breakfast still mattered.

That much before.

He cooks with great gusto and after it is cooked, he decides, though it smells delicious and the bacon is burnt to perfection, he cannot possibly eat it and so whooooosh, he slides it all straight from the frying pan into the ~~fire~~ bin. So, now he is back to pottering around with nothing to do. He decides to put up the door to her room. He feels compelled to do so. It is a debt he owes her.

It takes him almost the whole day. For a builder's son, this is shameful, but fixing things has never been one of his talents – something his father had chosen to make a habit of pointing out every chance he got.

'You're so queeny, son,' he would say with a snigger, 'delicate-like as a woman or a flowery man.'

That then – his inability to do what his father did for a living – had festered between them; a wound, opened, salted and shut, only to be reopened again. Once, when he was older, when he had finally mustered up enough courage to confront the source of his father's shame, he had retorted softly, 'Are you implying that gay men can't fix leaking roofs or if a man doesn't enjoy fixing leaking roofs, he is gay? Is that it? Is that what you are trying to say, Dad?'

His father had looked shocked at first, then angry, then hurt – it had always been one of his talents, this ability to look hurt on demand.

'Now, now,' he said placatingly, 'no need to be so sensitive, son... touchy-like as a woman or one of them flowery men...' and then he had laughed heartily, at his talentless son, or at his own humour or at how one enabled the other in such an obliging manner.

And like that, like the head of a king cobra, it rose again and again, that old familiar feeling of shame. There it was, just there, anywhere you looked, anywhere, everywhere, starting from childhood following him into youth, into manhood. Never ending, like a circle, inside his father.

So many layers of shame, so much depth.

1) the older man's shame at how his own life had turned out
   or how it hadn't
   recognising it
   (self-shame)

2) trying to rid himself of it
   of the feeling of feeling shame
   by stirring shame
   (vengeful shame)

3)   shaming the thing that was easiest to shame
and *him* allowing it to happen
allowing his father to do this to him
realising he was being shamed, realising why
but still *becoming* ashamed
(guilty shame)

4)   then in time growing weary of it
trying to fight back
to shame his father back
(retaliatory shame)

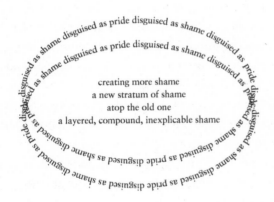

creating more shame
a new stratum of shame
atop the old one
a layered, compound, inexplicable shame

And now, because of his incapacity to do so earlier, because of
the circle of shame, his daughter has her door back after she
is dead.

Barthes
'As soon as someone dies, frenzied construction of the future
(shifting furniture, etc.): futuromania.'[48]

Him

His daughter's talent – her bar-one talent, which was not, like her other talents, an ordinary talent, but quite an extraordinary talent (meaning superlative, meaning momentous, meaning remarkable) – was in acting.

She had been a wonderful actress already at fourteen, star of every school play since the age of five. Birthday presents had been trips to the West End. Christmas presents, too. Musicals were her favourite. He had loved taking her to the theatre, loved watching her eyes light up. He imagined she was imagining herself on that stage.

Yes, she wanted nothing more than to be a 'real' actress (famous, accomplished) which seemed not improbable, being that she was naturally gifted with an expressive face, a good ear, a good voice, the ability to move her body in dance and a rather uncanny flair for the dramatic.

She took to spending hours in front of the mirror honing her art, contorting her Rita Hayworth face into a whole range of expressions and emotions. Practising her faces.

He steps into her bedroom, now with its door back on; he stands in front of the mirror where she used to practise her faces. He practises his own:

Happy Daddy

Funny Daddy

Angry Daddy

Sad Daddy

So-stupendously-sad Daddy.

He wants to cry but watching himself do it is much too much of an event.

Barthes
'The face of Garbo is an Idea, that of Hepburn, an Event.'[49]

Him
He has become an obsessive maker of lists; a convert, a believer. He makes another list. It is titled 'The Never List'. Another masterpiece.

The Never List

I Will Never...
Help her with homework
Take off her bedroom door
Put it back on
Hear her laugh
Hold her
Watch her sleep
Look at her face
Listen to the sound of her voice
Cook her eggs and bacon
Disapprove of her boyfriend(s)
Befriend her husband
Dance at her wedding
Be a grandfather
Tell her I love her
Call her by her name

She Will Never...
Sit her GCSEs
Slam another door
Call me Daddy
Turn fifteen
Become a woman
See the Eiffel Tower lit up at night
Fall in love
Perform on Broadway
Or in the West End
Or anywhere
Watch another sunset
Or another sunrise
Get married
Be a mother
Lose a child

He adds more rows under the last row and leaves them blank to populate at a later time.

He cries and smudges the ink and the list is now destroyed.

Barthes
'No more I love you's.'[50]

Him
There's that day she was born.

His wife had been in labour for three days.

He remembers it clearly. He remembers it as the longest few hours of his life, peppered with moments of pride and horror. Yes, he remembers it clearly.

He is in the room with HER.

He is filled with a new-found respect for HER, for womankind. What SHE is doing, he could never do. Never. Not ever.

'Push, push,' the pair of incredible Nigerian midwives (Ebi and Oluchi) chant enthusiastically. They chant rhythmically, their bodies heaving, moving to their own indomitable beat.

'Push, push,' he chants with them, trying to be a helpful third. But he is out of sync. The beat they move to so naturally is lost on him.

He's not feeling very helpful is the problem. Truth of the matter is that he's feeling a little bit sick. It's empathy of course, SHE's in pain, he's watching HER *be* in pain, there's that. But it's also what he's seeing. No one tells you about what you're going to be seeing. It's not supposed to be about the man. Nothing ever is, but particularly not this event. Justifiably so.

The problem with the problem is that it is squarely his – he cannot talk to HER about it, he cannot talk to anyone about it, he cannot even talk to himself about it, meaning he doesn't comprehend it fully himself. He's always had it, this problem with intimacy, the supposedly no-limits nature of it, even if it is with people he loves. One time he had sex with his wife and it coincided, unbeknownst to either of them, with the start of HER monthly visit. This is before SHE was pregnant of course. One of the biggest benefits of pregnancy, according to his wife, was that the visitation stopped for a while.

Anyway, that whole episode had scarred him for life. He's ashamed to admit it, but that doesn't change how he had felt. He had washed his penis for days after, in a kind of pathological way. It wasn't HER fault, of course not. And he wasn't a small-minded person, it was a normal biological thing, he knows that, of course he does. But the trauma to a man of pulling out a penis covered in blood when you do not expect it is something one is never meant to express. It isn't considered politically correct. No, even harbouring such thoughts is wrong. Unempathetic, immoral, misogynistic. So, he tells nobody. There's a lot of that same stuff now. Also mixed in with other stuff. The nausea is overwhelming. But of course, he's not allowed to feel it, let alone say it. Would it be unforgiveable if he left the room?

There's a spurt of it now, a whole big giant glob of what belongs – surely – in the privacy of one's body.

'Oh fuck,' he thinks.

'OH FUCK,' SHE screams.

'It's a girl,' they say, handing him the glob.

And the nausea is replaced magically by an overwhelming love that lasts fourteen years.

He wants to go back again, to that time.

Barthes
'I encounter millions of bodies in my life; of these millions, I may desire some hundreds; but of these hundreds, I love only one.'[51]

Him
Outside the confines of his own mind, out in the world, there is a war raging.

It started some six months before his daughter died and has officially been named 'Operation Enduring Freedom' by the United States Government. Unofficially, it is known as the 'War in Afghanistan', which of course sounds far less morally compelling.

He understands the nuances of language, its political importance, its pathos.

Already in these past few months the war has caused between 1,300 and 8,000 'direct' deaths, 'direct' being defined in technical terms as those killed by bombs and missiles. Mathematics, as his dead daughter once pointed out, is not his thing, still he doesn't understand how the difference between the low count and the high count in this calculation could possibly be to the tune of 6,700 people. Nor how there are also deaths that are labelled 'indirect' deaths – a number more than twice the high end of the 'direct' range – 'indirect' being defined as caused by something other than bombs and missiles, which would include things like poverty, starvation, cold, drought or the Taliban. Also, the Americans, but just not (for clear and unbiased reporting purposes) in a 'direct' way.

Come to think of it, he fails to grasp the basic concept of an 'indirect' death, in that:

none of these people were 'directly' targeted

therefore

they couldn't possibly have been the enemy in any 'direct' way

therefore

they did not need to die to save the civilised world (the entire premise, as he understands it, of this war)

therefore

notwithstanding the inevitable collateral damage from any war, if the number of 'indirect' deaths could possibly be this high, it pointed, surely, to an extreme recklessness in the operation of the thing. Not to mention indifference, callousness and a complete and unapologetic lack of care.

With all this direct and indirect business, a true count of the death toll is impossible, they report on the news.

An American general famously says, '*You know* we don't do body counts.'

He, on the other hand, can do a body count. His body count is one. And, he wants to say to the American general, man to man, father to father, that even one is one too many times a man can afford to lose his child.

You know?

Barthes

'There is a time when death is an event, an ad-venture, and as such mobilizes, interests, activates, tetanizes. And then one day it is no longer an event, it is another *duration*, compressed, insignificant, not narrated, grim, without recourse: true mourning not susceptible to any narrative dialectic.'[52]

Him

They are meant to be religious people, a religious family. At least SHE is, HER side of the family. And his father of course. This is perhaps the only thing they have somewhat in common – his father and HERs – God providing a bridge to connect their otherwise unbridgeable worlds.

His own position on the matter, he thinks best not to express, but SHE knew, SHE learned, slowly, over time, that the loss inside him was something that could never again be found, that with his mother, all those years ago when he was only twelve, he had lost other things as well – innocence, faith, religion, God.

But still, he said nothing, made no complaint, went to church every single Sunday for all those years, for HER sake, for his daughter's, pretending to pray, feeling nothing, feeling like a fraud, but saying nothing, playing along, praying along.

It's been several weeks now since their daughter died, several weeks for them without church. 'We should go to mass,' his wife says, 'it'll help us in these dark times.' He nods.

They go together, just the two of them, like they used to after they got married, on all those Sundays, before their daughter happened. They see familiar faces, only they no longer have that familiarity that comes with familiar faces. These are faces that stop laughing when they see them (now parents-of-a-dead-child), stop speaking mid-sentence, turn fearful as if their own pleasure seems sinful around someone else's pain.

They walk on, pretending not to notice how the energy has shifted, squeeze into one of the pews, avoid stepping on feet, find themselves a couple of seats. Some people come by, touch their shoulders, tell them how sorry they are, their voices steady, almost pleasant, betraying that all-too-familiar tone, that repetitively rehearsed mixture of pity and awkwardness. The parents-of-a-dead-child respond politely; thank you, they say, thank you, you are all very kind.

Death makes an actor of everyone.

The priest hesitates when he sees them, but it is only a flicker. He is earnest, eager to spread God's message. He nods at them, stands at the pulpit, starts to read his sermon. 'This is Jeremiah 23:24,' he says. 'Can a man hide himself in secret places so that I cannot see him? declares the Lord. Do I not fill heaven and earth? declares the Lord.'

Father-of-a-dead-child raises his eyes, turns his head around, looks at the faces of the people sat behind him, expectant faces these, keen to understand the omnipotence of this benevolent God they are being told about. The priest presses on, offers his exegesis.

'Jeremiah asked a rhetorical question with an obvious answer; there is no place you can be where the Lord is not aware of your presence. God declares that He fills both Heaven and Earth and so there is nowhere – no dark and secret place – a man can go where he is hidden from Him. God is omnipresent. God is everywhere,' he concludes definitively.

Father-of-a-dead-child raises his hand.

The priest looks at him nervously. Mother-of-a-dead-child shifts uncomfortably next to him, clutches the folds of HER dress. SHE is ill-at-ease with HER other half, all these new things in him, the unpredictability, the volatility, the repressed anger of HER other half, HER now-literally-joined-together-by-the-world-in-sorrow other half.

'Yes, my son?' the priest enquires, his small eyes darting around like a little fish in a duck pond. This could be trouble, he's had experience with trouble, knows trouble when he sees it.

Father-of-a-dead-child puts his hand down. Opens his mouth and his manner is composed and his eyes are chilling. 'On the day my daughter died,' he says in a voice so calm, it is terrifying, 'in which fuck-hole was God?'

Barthes

'Horrible figure of mourning: acedia, hard-heartedness: irritability, impotence to love. Anguished because I don't know how to restore generosity to my life – or love. How to love?'[53]

Him

He is beginning to learn the texture of grief.

Barthes

'What kind of Lucifer created love and death at the same time?'[54]

Him

Sigmund the psychoanalyst said, 'The goal of all life is death.'

But Emily the poet said, 'Unable are the loved to die. For love is immortality.'

He is Sigmund. SHE is Emily.

'We've got to get her out! We've got to save her!' SHE says one day, rushing into the bedroom, clasping HER hands together, a strange light in HER green eyes.

He looks up at HER and his own eyes are sad. He says nothing. The thing is, he cannot fault HER, not entirely. The idea that the dead might not be dead, as in fully dead, permanently dead, forever dead, is a tantalising one. Entire cultures are built around the notion of the afterlife, a kind of blessed everlasting forever where our time on Earth is only a part of a much bigger whole. Also, entire industries. Cryogenics, taxidermy, Dolly the sheep. Capitalism, as he understands it, is never far behind – capitalising, as it were, on whatever it can find. Easy pickings.

'But,' SHE continues, and HER enthusiasm will not be quelled, 'what if they were wrong? What if she was just in a coma? My God! What if she is still just in a coma, buried all the way down there in that box? We've got to get her out! We've got to save her!'

How can he tell a woman who has lost so much already that if SHE doesn't check HERself, SHE could also lose HER mind?

Barthes

'...in the realm of love, futility is not a "weakness" or an "absurdity": it is a strong sign: the more futile, the more it signifies and the more it asserts itself as strength.'[55]

Him

He found his own mother hanging in her bedroom when he was twelve. He pushed open the slightly ajar door and there she was, dangling, naked, except for the three multicoloured silk scarves that she had carefully knotted together to make the noose that her now broken neck hung from.

Her eyes were open, a deep dark blue, still extraordinarily beautiful.

There was no note.

The dining table was set with three place settings and on the hob was a pot of pea and ham soup that filled the kitchen with a warm, comforting aroma.

His father returned home from the building site where he spent his days aiding in the construction of a brand-new, high-tech, state-of-the-art shopping mall and discovered his wife and child; the former hanging silently from the ceiling, the latter crouched silently under the bed.

'Call your mother,' he said, pulling his son out by the wrist so forcefully that the child broke his silence and yelped. 'Tell her dinner's ready.'

Then he went into the kitchen, ladled out three bowls of soup and said grace.

Even now, after all these years, his father continues to speak of his mother in the present tense, as if none of what happened had happened at all.

Barthes
'The measurement of mourning: eighteen months for mourning a father, a mother.'[56]

Him
He needs to get out, he is gagging for air.

'Why are you in your running gear?' SHE asks.

'I'm going for a run,' he replies truthfully.

'Our daughter is dead and you're going for a run?'

SHE does little to mask the vitriol and at first, he cannot make sense of it. Why, he wonders, should a desire to go running be grounds for a fight? But then, he realises, if you really want to, you can make anything into a fight.

But it is not the second part of HER sentence that gets him; the first half hits him like a blow to the head that sends him reeling and he has to steady himself before he is back on stable ground.

He takes off his running shoes like a chastised child, and as he unties his laces, he says it out loud, what SHE just said, he repeats HER words in his voice, he shouts them to himself. Correction: *at* himself.

'Our daughter is dead.'

Barthes

'A Buddhist Koan says: The master holds the disciple's head underwater for a long, long time; gradually the bubbles become fewer; at the last moment, the master pulls the disciple out and revives him: when you have craved truth as you crave air, then you will know what truth is.'[57]

Him

When the person who creates you and the person you create both die, what kind of arsehole does that make you?

Abominable life bookended by death

not to be or (to be or not to be)

That is the question, Prince Hamlet, that is the question.

(Infinitely more complicated than the original, as you will have noted).

(Lesson notes: Trauma is very ~~historical~~ hysterical.)

Barthes

'To whom could I put this question (with any hope of an answer)?'[58]

Him

Once, not that long ago, SHE was full of light. A year after their marriage, SHE had HER first book published and SHE was so happy, awash in the afterglow. HER happiness was infectious, spreading its radiance around like a brilliant, bountiful sun.

And him! There was no man more proud of his wife than him, on that glittering evening of HER book launch, the clink of glasses, the tinkle of laughter, and HER, looking ravishing in a long, gold dress that picked out the gold flecks in HER auburn hair and made HER quite literally shine. 'I'm only the husband,' he said to everyone all evening, 'the supporting act.'

'There's nothing else in the world I'd rather do,' SHE said later in bed, hugging him, hugging HERself, hugging the happiness between them, as if in doing that, it would stay in that space forever, it would never leave.

'This is just the beginning,' everyone said, 'the start of something great, now that you've got your foot in the door. You just need to run with it and it's yours, success after success.'

'You must be so proud,' they said to him, 'to be married to such a talented woman.'

And he *was*. He was proud. He was overjoyed. The happiest shadow the sun ever made.

SHE deserved it, he thought, HER happiness, HER every success. SHE wrote wonderfully, *wonderfully!* and SHE had worked so hard. Hours, days, months, years, years, years... four years spent in near isolation in the library on Euston Road with a laptop for company.

HER book was about a middle-aged woman trapped in a loveless marriage. He had been HER first reader. At first, not even a year into the marriage, he had grown alarmed at the prospect of a possible autobiographical angle. He had heard writers often subliminally project from their own lives. Was this about HER, about them, about what SHE thought lay ahead?

But SHE had only laughed at the suggestion. 'It's a work of fiction, baby. Other people's lives. None of it is true. Neither the people, nor their lives.'

The book did well, sold more copies than either of them had imagined. A runaway success, you could call it, followed by disappointment after disappointment as every subsequent attempt failed to make it past any editor's inbox.

'Not commercial enough,' explained the rejection letters politely.

'Not enough torque and bite.'

'Didn't connect completely with the characters.'

'Didn't fall totally in love with it.'

He didn't understand. SHE was a beautiful writer.

At first, SHE persevered past all the negativity. Didn't let it touch HER, kept HER head high and HER chin up.

'I will not give up. I am not a quitter,' SHE would say every morning on HER way to the library.

'Five hundred words today, good day. A thousand words today, champion day,' SHE would say in the evenings on HER way back.

But.

There is only so far you can keep going before it swallows you up, failure – you and everything else that's yours, your confidence, your morale and eventually your sanity.

But.

SHE was bold. SHE was brassy.

HER v. Failure: SHE won round one.

Then their daughter was born.

SHE threw HERself into raising her.

She needs me, SHE said.

A child needs a mother. Not a writer.

Their daughter became a project.

'Just until school.'

Almost

Five years passed.

In a whirlwind of domestic bliss.

Kisses, cuddles
Jigsaw puzzles
Bedtime stories, cocoa-milk
Bath-time, bubbles, still more cuddles
Baby's bum as smooth as silk
Burt's Bees? Yes please!
Rhyming classes, ballet classes
Gymboree, three days a week
Baby talking, baby walking, Daddy, Daddy, look at me
Clean shirts, clean house
Nothing ever not in place
Crème brûlée, banana bread
Everywhere, the smell of cake
And sex.
Never tired, strangely wired. Always in the mood for sex
Come on baby, love me deep
Love me in places I can't even see.

(HER appetite was voracious.)

(He was delighted.)

Freud said: Sex is the opposite of death.

Oh, SHE was the opposite of death.

SHE was alive.

He was alive.

Their daughter was alive.

This, he said, is LIFE.

I miss it, SHE announced one day, sobbing so hard SHE couldn't even speak.

Life. I miss my life.

(Wait. What? SHE was unhappy?)

I'm done being *this* person, SHE said with contempt.

Baking muffins and making tea.

I have a degree

(from Oxford, too).

I need to be a writer.

I need to be me.

It's great to have you back, the pushy agent said. I read the manuscript you sent me! It's too good!

Too good. Too good…

'Fiction is subjective,' said one rejection letter.

'I'm going to have to pass,' said another.

'Couldn't identify with the voice.'

'Couldn't curl up with the characters.'

HER v. Failure: SHE lost round two.

SHE didn't even attempt round three.

SHE fired HER agent, threw away HER laptop and stopped writing.

SHE lost interest: in life, in HERself, in him entirely, in their daughter partially.

From him, this profound and persistent melancholy first elicited sympathy, then impatience, then eventually resignation. Eventually, that is, when SHE started to go to sleep with other people's novels, underlining sections with bright red ink, marking them out with asterisks and stars so that SHE could be inspired by ideas for a book SHE was never going to write.

Barthes
'The lover's fatal identity is precisely: I am the one who waits.'[59]

Him
There's the day he takes his daughter to the seaside. SHE isn't there, it's just him and her.

Her mother doesn't want to come; it's too cold, SHE says, too windy.

He understands. When it comes to The English Seaside, almost everyone is a fair-weather friend.

It is in the summer joys of the seaside... fairground rides and ice-cream cones and happy kids bobbing around the waves in underwear and how it feels to feel the sun on one's bare arms and the colour and the sweetness of the English strawberries and the strains of laughter in the air and the live band singing terrible versions of U2... it is in all this that these places have any meaning at all.

In the winter, all that becomes a kind of distant rolling fog in someone's mind. One need only step out of one's car in front of the seaside shops selling candy floss (pink, blue) and life-size balloons of animated characters (swollen, distorted), alongside condoms (flavoured, textured), first-aid kits and Arsenal t-shirts (small, medium, large), in the middle (smack-bang) of November, to realise with a kind of horror, gosh, it is *cold*, it is *windy*, it is utterly uncomfortable and totally depressing and why – again please – am I here?

So, he understands HER reluctance to come.

But the cold has never bothered him or his daughter in the way it bothers his wife, her mother. One of those strange genetic things, he thinks, that you can trace back definitively to one parent, definitively not to the other. So, he goes, just him and his daughter, for a day by the sea in the sad greyness of winter.

And they walk on the cold pebbly beach, side by side, with their thick down jackets and their hoodies pulled over their heads, and they eat their ice-cream cones (vanilla for him, strawberry for her), despite the wind, despite the chill, and the English sky is painted English grey and so is the sea, but they talk and they laugh and he feels he could listen to it forever, this sound of his daughter's laughter.

And then she kicks off her shoes and her socks and rolls up her jeans and runs towards the ocean, meeting it, the icy water kissing her pale toes, then her ankles, then her knees. 'Come in Daddy, come in, it's sooooo cold!' she yells, and her voice carries a marvel and that marvel carries in the wind.

And he shakes his head – no chance! – and yet he finds his feet moving towards her, mysteriously, and then his shoes are off, and so are his socks and his toes are in the water, clear and icy cold, right next to hers.

He is filled then, in that moment, his entire being, with a love and also simultaneously a fear, and both the love and the fear are equal, and both the love and the fear are so strong and so overpowering that he can barely comprehend any of it at all. Only, he retains the vague awareness that without the love, there would be no fear and without the fear, there would be no love.

He wants to go back again, to that place.

Barthes
'Engulfment is a moment of hypnosis.'[60]

Him

There is only one other time he remembers seeing his mother naked. He has come home from school one afternoon; she is nowhere in the house, and then he sees her naked by the shrubs at the back, watering the roses. In one hand she holds open a Philip Larkin book. In the other, she is holding the tip of the bright green garden hose that runs between her legs, clutched bizarrely between her thighs.

He needs to bring her back in, that much he knows. She isn't well, his mother, and he needs to bring her back into the house. He goes out. She doesn't see him immediately and for a while he stands quietly, unsure of what to do, how to make his presence known, he stands silently by the holly tree so full of dark red berries that look delicious but are deadly if consumed, and watches her as she reads her book while watering those peach-coloured blushing roses and humming a tune, doing all three at the same time.

'Oh, hello darling,' she says when she finally looks up with her beautiful blue eyes and spots him, and she smiles, a big, happy smile, pausing momentarily her reading, her humming, but not her watering. 'How was school?'

Over in the top left window of the house on the other side of the fence, old Mrs Harper shakes her head before lowering her blinds to keep the devil out.

Barthes

'A delirium, however, does not exist unless one wakens from it (there are only retrospective deliriums).'[61]

Him

Another dissembling thing happens. He meets a friend of his daughter's, one of the blonde girls who she'd been with on that night. He bumps into her in the root vegetables aisle of the grocery store. He is looking for, and unable to find, a very specific variety of potato that is about halfway down the list SHE has given him. This is important to HER, this distinction in potato varietals, one can never be mistaken for another; he knows this from past experience.

She's a nice girl, the friend of his daughter's whom he meets. 'Oh hello,' she says in surprise when they bump into each other, addressing him by his last name, prefixing it politely with 'Mister', and their eyes connect but he can see the momentary flicker of panic in hers, for he was exactly how she had addressed him, sure, but he was *also* so-and-so's daddy, but no longer is he so-and-so's daddy, and that explains the panic. He understands this in her, more than he understands his own panic, in him, so he says hello back – very quickly – then abandons the potatoes and rushes out of the store as fast as he can, like a thief or a madman. He would rather feign forgetfulness and bear the brunt of his wife's ire than try and rationalise the panic that courses through his veins like a kind of electric current, because that could have been his daughter, easily could have been his daughter there, right there, standing by the wrong kind of potatoes greeting someone else's daddy, but it's not, and it will never be.

And for that, he is jealous, jealous of the girl, jealous that she is shopping for potatoes, jealous of her life, and he hates himself for his jealousy of her.

There. That's his panic explained, then.

He misses his daughter. That is all.

Barthes

'As a jealous man, I suffer four times over: because I am jealous, because I blame myself for being so, because I fear that my jealousy will wound the other, because I allow myself to be subject to a banality: I suffer from being excluded, from being aggressive, from being crazy, and from being common.'[62]

Him

Two months have passed.

For him, it has become a different kind of grief that can no longer be expressed by gestures.

No, by now it is fully internalised, the kind of grief you cannot rid yourself of, that sits in your gullet like a stone suspended on a string, choking you each time you swallow (your sorrow).

This is not about 'letting go'.

This is not about 'moving on'.

This is not about 'time healing one's wounds'.

This is none of those ~~bullshit~~ helpful phrases that ~~arseholes~~ kind and compassionate people throw at you when they are trying to be ~~arseholey~~ kind and compassionate.

There is no language for this sort of thing.

This is only something trying to happen, this is searching for some semblance of normality, this is searching for some way to carry on breathing.

Barthes

'Does being able to live without someone you loved mean you loved her less than you thought...?'[63]

Him

He's never done nothing for as long as he can remember. He's bored and numb. Numbed by the boredom of grief. Also bored by the numbness of grief. Both equally applicable.

He turns off all the lights and watches a movie by himself. It is a 1948 black-and-white Italian film called *Bicycle Thieves* and the story is about a poor father who scours through post-WWII Rome in search of his stolen bicycle. Without the bicycle, he will lose his job; without his job, he will not be able to provide for his family. So, it is crucial, this bicycle, the need to find this bicycle, the quest for this object without which there is nothing.

He watches the movie with great interest. He finds a kind of universality in the story, a sentiment he can intimately relate to. For instance, he could be the father, trapped in a kind of futile quest.

Yes, he decides, while his fingers search the bowl for the last of the popcorn hidden amidst all the unpopped kernels and (another futile quest) finding none, reach instead for the unopened pack of cigarettes:

He is Antonio Ricci, the father.

The war is the one inside his head.

The bicycle is his daughter.

The thief is God.

The bicycle will never be found. Neither will justice.

He feels ashamed then, equating his own horror to that of WWII, the scale of that terrible, global event. And the fact that it is over, but it will never be over, if you think about it in a certain way. That is always the way with war.

He thinks then about the current one, not a world war, but still a war, raging in the desert between two wildly asymmetric powers.

And the one inside his head.

And the one he is fighting almost daily with HER.

How many wars, he thinks, can you fight at the same time?

Barthes

'The subject painfully identifies himself with some person (or character) who occupies the same position as himself in the amorous structure.'[64]

Him

If he looks at a calendar and puts a red cross on the days they've had an argument and a blue tick on the days they haven't, the calendar would be a sea of red.

There are tea stains on the cups, SHE complains, disgusting! Creases on the sheets, shoes in all the wrong places, muddy too, the grass needs mowing, the hedges need trimming, the laundry needs putting away, the car needs cleaning, the toilet seat is up again, yes, up again, books, books *everywhere*, poetry, too much poetry, too much Emily Dickinson, too much Robert Frost and Poe and Yeats. Plath too. Too much Suicidal Sylvia. Too much music as well, all this unnecessary joy, too much Beethoven's Fifth, too much Aaron Goldberg trio, way, way, too much cigarette smell. Plus, he's forgotten to buy the potatoes.

It has nothing to do with their daughter.

It has everything to do with their daughter.

Barthes

'I am in mourning for an object which is itself in mourning.'[65]

Him

There are so many dimensions of grief.

Barthes

'I do not know that the word "suffering" expresses no suffering and that, consequently, to use it is not only to communicate nothing but even, and immediately, to annoy, to irritate (not to mention the absurdity).'[66]

Him

He wonders if there is a time...

When someone will say something funny and he will laugh again.

Or

When the

> shape and sound of a word or
> the genius of Bach or of
> Miles Davis's 'So What' or the
> WONDER
> of
> Wordsworth's daffodils
> (Larkin's deprivation)

will gladden him again.

When things will have beauty again because they can, and they should, and they need to.

Barthes

'Like love, mourning affects the world – and the worldly – with unreality, with importunity. I resist the world, I suffer from what it demands of me, from its demands. The world increases my sadness, my dryness, my confusion, my irritation, etc. The world depresses me.'[67]

Him

He used to be romantic once.

Once, when he was romantic, like he used to be, he made the whole place dark and lit aromatic candles and played Paula Cole on the old-fashioned turntable he had been given by his father, who in turn had been given it by a famous Indian artist whose house his father had renovated on Curzon Street because it was surplus to the artist's needs and also because the artist had a new mistress who was thirty years his junior and preferred Napster before it was legally shut down. Anyway, now the turntable was his and so he played 'Feelin' Love' on it. Also, he scattered rose petals on the bed in the shape of a heart. But SHE had received a rejection that day from a publisher SHE had hung HER hopes on and SHE said SHE didn't feel like it, so he picked up the rose petals one by one and fed them to the dog.

In a parallel version, SHE saw what he had done and that immediately changed HER mood and they got completely naked and made beautiful love and the dog scratched on the door wondering what the heck the humans were up to now, and then when she convinced herself that those horrible and seemingly unending noises were not, definitely not, from pain, but also that the humans were not, definitely not, going to come out and play with her anytime soon, she got bored and went to find a bone to chew on.

He can't remember now which version was the real one.

Barthes

'Union: Dream of total union with the loved being.'[68]

Him

He goes for a run when SHE is out, when he is safe from HER contempt, from HER judgement.

He jogs to the trim trail, a six-mile loop round Kenwood House lake.

It's just like old times. Only it isn't.

He's always been an able runner. Long legs, swift. He picks up speed. His feet make no sound. He glides.

It's turned chilly again in the last few days, an unexpected weather pattern in June.

There's beauty in the cold air. The heath is wild; the lake is still.

Strange shapes sit on it, unmoving, ghostlike.

Logs, stumps, blown in by a long-ago wind.

There's a flock of egrets, long-legged and lily-white.

Huddled together in a small oasis.

A giant frog leaps off a lily pad.

An unexpected patch of green in the middle of the water.

It lands next to the egrets, surprising them.

Even as he watches, one takes flight, gliding gracefully in the air, then descending a few minutes later, on a floating piece of driftwood.

The bird looks confused, its perch sailing.

And it on top, slipping and sliding.

The log gives way suddenly, without warning, breaking off in chunks.

There is a great flapping of wings; a collective high-pitched cry.

He thinks to himself, how precious life is, how fragile.

And then he thinks of the little girl who both makes him glad that she was born and wish that he were dead.

Barthes

'What affects me most powerfully: mourning in layers – a kind of sclerosis.

[Which means: no depth. Layers of surface – or rather, each layer: a totality. Units.]'[69]

Him

Layers and layers of missing.

    Like one of those Russian babushka dolls.

    Missing that you think is over and then keep finding more.

    Missing that comes up in the most unexpected times.

    When he is walking down the street; when he is speaking to someone,

    Mid stride; mid conversation.

    Or when he is in a crowded shop.

    Buying bread.

    Or buying washing-up liquid.

    Or not buying potatoes.

    Or reading the newspaper.

    Or buttering his toast.

    Or looking at his wife,

    And seeing his daughter.

Barthes

'Paradoxically (since people say: work, amuse yourself, see friends) it's when we're busy, distracted, sought out, exteriorized, that we suffer most. Inwardness, calm, solitude makes us less miserable.'[70]

Him

On the other side of the television screen, in a land so foreign it could as well be a scene from a movie, the war still rages.

People feeding off people.

Countries feeding off countries.

He and SHE, feeding off each other.

Grief, feeding off them.

Barthes

'...the book creates meaning, the meaning creates life.'[71]

Him

He would never have said anything at all, he was doing so well with that, he thought, this business of not saying anything, but how long is it possible, how long can a man bite his tongue before he cuts it and out comes that bloody scream?

The thing is, SHE started to say things. Randomly and unprovoked. And then SHE did it again. And again and again and again. So then he began to say things he never would have said, never wanted to say, never thought would say. Maybe everyone has a bleeding tongue just waiting to let rip.

SHE says, 'You've turned into your father.'

He says, 'Do you think drinking yourself to death will bring her back to life?'

And SHE says, 'How dare you? How *dare* you? This is not your classroom, Professor.'

And he says, 'Don't. Please don't start with that again.'

And SHE only shrugs.

And he says, 'How can we do this, how can we get through this, if you won't even talk to me?'

And SHE positions HER chin at that particular angle and HER eyes flash an enigmatic forest green and SHE says, 'Okay baby. Let's talk. What would you like to talk about? Your dead poets and your dead philosophers? Your dead mother? Or your dead daughter?'

And he looks at HER face and he sees that there is nothing anymore in there that he recognises, nothing tender, nothing soft, a face that is impenetrable, impossible.

'Are you blaming me?' he says incredulously. 'Are you blaming me for her death?'

'Do you blame your father for your mother's death?'

'This is not about my mother,' he says tiredly, 'this is *not* about her.'

'Why weren't you there?' SHE finally asks – the question SHE has not asked, SHE now asks, expected, yet unexpected, throwing HER off, throwing him on, SHE slips it into the space between them, shifting it like a syncopated beat, and the relief and the rhythm and the hurt and the guilt drift to the ceiling and spread themselves out around the room, languidly, as if in no particular hurry. The blow of a saxophone on the downstairs record player breaks the silence, music from another time, complicated music, music rife with an illicit, intricate bitterness masquerading as something beautiful.

'Why weren't you there when she got off that bus?'

Then they have it out, two boxers in a ring, gloves off and good luck both. And it must make them feel better, exposing each other's secret vulnerabilities like this, because they go on for a very long time. And the only thing they agree on in the end, in a stony, impassive, almost clinical manner, is that they have said enough things for a lifetime's worth of saying things and that they should now, both for the love of God and for the sake of their dead child, stop. Which – because the language of words can be like that if you're not careful – means one thing to him and an altogether different thing to HER.

Barthes

'The true act of mourning is not to suffer from the loss of the loved object; it is to discern one day, on the skin of the relationship, a certain tiny stain, appearing there as the symptom of a certain death: for the first time I am doing harm to the one I love, involuntarily, of course, but without panic.'[72]

Him

He becomes a foreigner inside his own house.

Wanderer. Traveller. Nomad.

No-mad.

Also, yes-mad. Yes. Mad. Deeply crazy. Totally insane.

He has been inside a classroom his whole life, first as a student, then as a teacher; without it, without his classroom, his poetry, he is lost.

Come back, they said, when you're over it.

He breaks the sentiment down.

'It' is proving to be very mysterious. He cannot figure it out. Over what? he wants to ask all those clever men – over the top, over the counter, over the moon, over the hills and far away?

He's smoking too much. Eating too many damn biscuits.

A man in freefall.

Hoping for soft ground. Finding only the biscuit jar.

He screws opens the lid, grabs two more sickly sweet

chocolate-covered Penguins, turns on the telly. Flips to the news. There is more trouble in the Middle East. Whispers of a new war. Separate, evidently, from the ongoing war. The ongoing one is in Afghanistan. The target of this new one is rumoured to be Iraq, an altogether different country. On the other side, the 'good' side, fighting both, is the great and the United States of America. Supported by its ever-loyal sidekick, the United Kingdom of Great Britain. Because that's what allies do. Fight on the same side. Even in a different war.

Although, to him, it seems like the same war. A war of power.

The newsreader with the perfect teeth attempts to demystify the situation for the benefit of her viewers. *If*, she prefaces with practised caution, *if* the situation were to unfold... It has not, she emphasises, unfolded, neither is there any indication that it *will* unfold. Only, it *might* unfold. The demystification, therefore, deals with the possibility of the situation, rather than the situation itself. Still, it is important to explore all possibilities. Duties and obligations of the media; it is why they exist.

Hence, the special report:

The president of the United States, she reports, feels convinced that Iraq, that tiny country in the Middle East run by a moustached dictator of the evilest kind, is the site of large secret stockpiles of weapons of mass destruction that could destroy the civilised world as we know it. It is incumbent, therefore, in the opinion of the president, for the leaders of the civilised world to form an alliance and nip this in the bud, i.e. to take the bull by the horns, i.e. to declare war against that tiny country in a unified mission to save the civilised world from these large secret stockpiles of dangerous weapons.

She keeps referring to it as I-rack. This irritates him. He wonders why people cannot train their tongues to pronounce words as they should be pronounced. Whoever declared that proper nouns can be pronounced any which way, he thinks, was probably called Bob.

He also wonders about other things, logistical things. Such as the question of how such large stockpiles of dangerous weapons could be so cleverly hidden for so long. He thinks of all the possible places they could be hidden. If he was a dictator of a small country, where would he hide them, he wonders, these large previously unheard-of stockpiles of dangerous weapons?

Would they be buried, unbeknownst to ordinary people, in the soil under their homes? Hidden in an underground maze of copper sewage pipes? Tucked away inside the unused bathtubs within the unused bathrooms of his own presidential palace?

On that note, he decides to have a bath.

He goes up the stairs and into the bathroom. Runs the bath. Takes his clothes off slowly, first his shirt, then his trousers, last his underpants. Carefully appraises his naked body in the mirror while the bath is filling. He is neither happy nor unhappy with what he sees. He looks middle-aged, he thinks, which is as much as one can hope for when one is middle-aged.

Still very little flab. Still some muscle. Bit round the tummy could do with some firmness. Damn those Penguins. He needs some sun, he's way too pale. He hasn't been on holiday in ages. Just sitting on a beach in France or somewhere with a book and a frosted glass of something cold and highly intoxicating. Carefree and careless.

On a whim, he makes his way out of the bathroom, the

bedroom, then he is down the wooden stairs and in his kitchen. Naked, like that.

There's no one else in the house. SHE is out with HER mum. His daughter is dead.

There is a squirrel in the garden. It stares at him through the glass pane with its big, brown, surprisingly fearless eyes. He wonders what the squirrel makes of what it sees, of the thin, balding man with his pale exposed backside, standing alone, staring back at it. Carefree and careless.

They have accumulated, he notices, turning his eyes away from the squirrel, a rather impressive wine collection. This is thanks to the various visitors. He wonders how long it will take HER to go through the lot at HER current, rather extraordinary pace.

He picks out a Miraval Rosé because the sound of its name reminds him of a French sea. Turquoise blue, glittering under a big yellow French sun.

Then, armed with the bottle, one glass, two bars of chocolate and precisely three cigarettes (self-control, must exhibit self-control, must do, yes), he goes back upstairs, places everything carefully on the plastic rim of the tub and lowers himself into the water.

He grimaces. He's made it way too hot.

He pours the wine, smells it. It's a high-quality wine; whoever gave it to them didn't skimp, he can tell just from the smell. He takes a sip. Begins to soap himself, starting from his toes, working his way up, lifting each leg as he does it, lifting straight up, ninety degrees. He's impressed he can still do that, that he has the flexibility, the agility, the movement, to do leg raises like that.

He smokes the three cigarettes back-to-back between washing one testicle and the next.

Then picks up the bottle again and pours himself some more.

There's a word for mixing excessive amounts of alcohol with excessive amounts of chocolate: it's called 'bingeing'.

He hereby declares himself successfully binged.

He feels the urge to sing. He's a pretty terrible singer. Despite that, despite his no-sense of melody, he loves to sing.

There is no one around to hear him. This fact emboldens him.

He starts to sing.

'*When I was a little boy*
I was very full of joy
Now, I'm old and hairy
And very, very scary'

Surprisingly, he is singing rather well. More wine.

'*Halleluiah Halleluiah*
Halleluiah Halleluiah'

he sings – high, low, high, low – when the bathroom door opens towards him.

Motherfucker! he thinks, he didn't lock the door.

SHE stands there a moment. SHE looks distraught. He looks at HER, opens his mouth, but still SHE is just standing, not speaking, just watching him while he sits in the tub. His silence and HER silence. Pure, perfect silence. Then the silence mixes with the steam and the fake-sweetness of the bubble bath and the slightly sour smell of his man-ness and the acrid fumes of cigarette smoke and the floral aroma of the high-quality wine and all this takes the edge off past displays of lies and betrayal and abandonment and guilt.

'I'm singing,' he says.

SHE says nothing.

'Changed up the words,' he says. 'On purpose I mean.' He smiles sheepishly. 'Just a thing I do.'

Still, silence.

'Sometimes, I mean. I do it sometimes. Not every time.'

'Why didn't you lock the door?' SHE asks quietly. In his opinion, a very good question.

He shrugs.

The qi in the little bathroom shifts.

It is sexy now, provocative.

HER eyes gleam and so do his.

Do you? they ask each other, those four eyes – Do you dare?

PART III: AND THEN THERE WERE SEVEN

Him

(Deus ex machina.)

It's been five months exactly.

He is reading the newspaper. He is reading about the war. More violence, more blood, more gunshots and bombs, more children being killed or maimed or orphaned, more uncounted/unaccounted bodies (see, *see* what language can do, how guilefully meaning can shift).

He is pondering the scale of all this human horror when SHE asks him to leave.

He would like to say it comes as a shock because it seems both the appropriate reaction to have and the appropriate thing to say.

But there is nothing appropriate about any of this, so.

Truthfully, he feels strangely relieved. Knowing it was coming, *waiting* for it to come, *wondering* when it would come, the anticipation of anticipating, the expectation of expecting – all that was so much harder.

This seems almost like a release. He makes a noise and it sounds like an orgasm.

'You are revolting,' SHE says in disgust.

Barthes

'A mandarin fell in love with a courtesan. "I shall be yours," she told him, "when you have spent a hundred nights waiting

for me, sitting on a stool, in my garden, beneath my window."
But on the ninety-ninth night, the mandarin stood up, put his
stool under his arm, and went away.'[73]

Him

We need time, SHE said, we need space.

Two things, he feels, that come as a kind of epiphany to all
unhappy couples in the moment of realisation of their unhappiness.

Happy couples don't bother with time and space. What
trifling things are space and time to them. Space, for the happy
couple, is superfluous; a lifetime insufficient.

Not so them; so SHE said.

And then? After time? After space? What then?

Ah! But then! After the abstract nouns have done their
thing, in creeps the pesky verb: to think.

'We need space, we need time. To think.'

(Voilà, says Barthes, wherever he is. More mythologies.)

A telling verb, 'to think', very illuminating on the
psychological state of the human being doing the action.

For example, have you ever heard of any happy couple
saying, 'This morning, we are going to get up and think'?

He's afraid the answer is no.

Only unhappy couples and philosophers think.

Happy couples laugh and make love.

We do not need time, he wants to tell HER. We do not need
space. We only need for our daughter not to have died.

He's gagging to tell HER.

But he doesn't.

He simply nods and agrees.

Time, yes

Space, yes
Think, yes. Yes.

Barthes

'Annulment: Explosion of language during which the subject manages to annul the loved object under the volume of love itself: by a specifically amorous perversion, it is love the subject loves, not the object.'[74]

Him

He feels a philosophical peacefulness.

Up those familiar wooden stairs he goes and begins to pack his things. A kind of automatism kicks in. He opens out an old suitcase on the bed. The bed. Their bed. As always, it's perfectly made, the sheets starched, the pillows, different colours and sizes, elaborately arranged. It looks like a show bed in a bed showroom. Beautiful, untouched. The bed he's shared with HER every night for nineteen years, touching HER skin, hearing HER breathe, smelling HER smell. Entering sleep after entering HER. Well, sometimes, this last one.

He frowns. Had he known it was going to be his last night, perhaps he would have done things differently. Gone to bed a bit earlier in the evening. Lingered on a bit longer in the morning. Touched HER toes with his own. Talked or something.

Shouldn't farewells be marked in some way, by some word or exquisite gesture – memorialised?

He begins to hum a tune, an old tune, one SHE'd loved, one they'd danced to in a different life. For some reason humming it now makes him feel good.

Slowly, meticulously, he folds and then arranges his things in little piles next to the suitcase. T-shirts in one pile, shirts in another, trousers, shorts, underwear, socks, shoes, miscellaneous ties, scarfs, gloves. He puts half of everything into the suitcase, the other half he throws into a large bin bag to dispose of on his way out. For some reason this also makes him feel good.

He looks at his belongings in the suitcase. It seems funny that everything one can truly lay claim to fits, if you really want, into one half of a single suitcase.

The suitcase shuts easily. So different from all the times they've gone on holiday, when they've shared a suitcase, when SHE's had to sit on it, first on one side, then on another, giggling the whole time at the look of extreme concentration on his face while he zipped the thing shut under HER. 'You look constipated,' SHE would laugh. Which wasn't funny. But this is. This is funny. That you take more stuff when you go away for ten days than when you go away forever – that's funny. Oh, it's funny, whether you look at it right side up or upside down.

And now, he's done. He takes a long breath, then a long look around. He straightens the sheets. He knows they will be touching HER skin, and therefore, they must be perfect.

Barthes
'The gift is contact, sensuality: you will be touching what I have touched, a third skin unites us.'[75]

Him
He wonders if there is any great good that is meant to come out of this.

There is a photograph of his daughter on the wall outside

their bedroom, enlarged, framed, like one tends to do with photographs of one's children, make them into paintings, works of art of no value to anyone but you. She is smiling, his daughter, in the photograph, looking down at a tiny Tubby she holds in her arms, and he sees it suddenly, like a kind of boring aphorism in an all-too-familiar story, he sees her mother in her.

At some point, in a normal life, there would have been a brief and beautiful period of 'crossing over', when the girl would have looked almost a woman and the woman would have looked still a girl and time would seem to have stopped, and they would have appeared almost the same, two versions of the same person, become and becoming.

He sees this in the photograph, this inevitability which is never to be, he sees it in his daughter's green eyes and the bounce and texture of her hair and the forward arch of her neck as she looks down at the tiny weak-hearted dog, and the smattering of the freckles on her nose, that she hated, that her mother also hates in HERself, on HER own nose.

And now, he will leave behind both the photograph and the original likeness of its image. *Memento mori.*

He wonders if, when he stops seeing HER, he will stop missing *her.*

He wonders if *this* is the great good.

Barthes

'A photograph is always invisible, it is not it that we see.'[76]

Him

When he goes downstairs, SHE is already gone. This also, is not a surprise – SHE has always hated goodbyes.

In the past, when he travelled occasionally for conferences and things, SHE would always cry. It wasn't the attachment to him as much as a sentimentality SHE attached to people leaving, an uncertainty, an almost-fear that could be traced back, all the way back, almost to a science, to HER own childhood fears, to HER own father disappearing for weeks and months on business, to parts of the world SHE had never been to and could not name, leaving HER alone, leaving HER mother alone, busy making money, busy making love, busy trying to own the world, and to embrace it, too, the world and all its secrets and all its sadness and all its pagan eroticism. HER mother had learned to accept his masculine urges. She had learned to live with the loneliness. Which is to say, she had not died from it.

'I'm only going to be gone two days,' he would laugh, 'think of it as a break!' But SHE'd never find that funny, only shake HER head and continue crying, standing on the steps until the taxi drove away, until, as he watched HER from the rear window, SHE became smaller and smaller, and then disappeared from sight.

Eventually, he stopped making light of it. There is in some people, he realised, a certain emptiness that can never be filled. He knew all about that – what he already knew existed inside him, in time he recognised inside HER.

He stands now on these same steps.

He exhales. The breath comes out ragged, uneven.

He is slightly surprised at how matter-of-fact this whole thing has been, how banal.

There should be, should there not, some deep emotion surrounding such things. It's what the novels say, the movies.

All this turmoil, all this angst. But he feels nothing. No turmoil. No angst.

Then again, he knows why.

This is no novel, no movie. This is real life. The emotion has already been spent. And all that remains now is its absence, that familiar emptiness, inside him, inside HER. In the fantasy that coupling their individual emptiness would somehow fill them both.

There is a reason this is never mentioned in novels, in movies. Banal never sells.

Barthes

'It is my desire I desire, and the loved being is no more than its tool.'[77]

Him

One talks about the relative strength of a relationship (as if it were medicine or a tall glass of gin and tonic).

'They had a strong relationship,' one may say about someone-and-someone-else. 'Oh, theirs was not so strong,' one may say about some-other-someone-and-their-someone-else.

It must have some truth, he has to admit, when you consider why some relationships seem able to endure the most gruelling of tests while others break down so easily at the first possible sign of duress.

What then, he wonders, is the currency of a successful partnership? What *is* a strong relationship?

The truth is that you never think it won't last. You don't even think that it may not last. After all, there's love. Of course there is.

But here's a question nobody ever asks: Is there enough? (Love) (Drugs) (Gin)

Barthes

'I thought I was suffering from not being loved, and yet it is because I thought I was loved that I was suffering.'[78]

Him

(1) He remembers meeting HER for the first time.

It was at a party at a friend's house, a fellow PhD student in the Humanities department. He noticed HER straight away, HER walk, the way SHE moved, HER hair, HER provocativeness, HER expensive clothes. Also, HER mystery, HER figure, HER unreachability, HER eyes. Someone else's date. Someone like that is always someone else's date. After a while, they dimmed all the lights and the dancing started – intimate and indecent or faraway and foolish. Depending on the type of person one was. SHE was the first type; he, of course, was the second. After the dancing, they sat in a circle on the floor playing drinking games, and every now and then, he would look up and see HER date's arm around HER shoulders and HER green eyes looking not at HER date but at *him* with a mixture of coyness and flirtation that he found, in turns, and sometimes at the same time, both deceitful and magnificent.

Later that same night, they'd bumped into each other accidentally in front of the bathroom; he was coming out, SHE was waiting to go in. For some inexplicable reason, SHE'd found that frightfully funny.

This girl can laugh, he remembered thinking as he went to bed that night, and the thought of HER laughing had made him smile in his sleep.

(2) He remembers their first date.

He'd taken HER to watch an open-air movie on the rooftop of a shopping mall in North London. There were deck chairs and blankets, fairy lights above and a large screen in front. Tickets included popcorn, one drink and comfy blankets in case the wind picked up. He handed HER a glass of red wine in a plastic cup as the opening credits rolled.

'*Casablanca*?' SHE asked, lips apart, eyebrows raised, looking amused.

'Why?' he said anxiously. 'You don't like it?'

'No, no, not at all. Everybody likes *Casablanca*.' SHE looked around. 'This place is nice... quaint.'

They'd held hands under the stars.

When Ingrid Bergman and Humphrey Bogart first kissed, he tried to kiss HER, too, and then a few times after that, but each time, he'd been too nervous.

'Oh, just do it already,' SHE said, and then kissed him. SHE tasted of red wine and popcorn.

When he dropped HER home that night to HER big house on HER expensive street in SW1, SHE said, 'You are so different from anybody I ever thought I'd go out with, but boy, do I fancy you.'

(3) He remembers the day they got married.

The old stone church, sunlight streaming in through the stained glass, afternoon rainbows on every wall.

HER family impeccably dressed (deep-pocketed, well-heeled) on one side still wearing the same expression of disbelief as they had when SHE had first introduced him to them; his father on the other side looking awkward and uncomfortable in a suit he'd worn twice before, once at his own wedding, once at his wife's funeral. Two worlds meant never to meet.

'Don't do it, son,' his father had said on the morning of the wedding, outside the church. 'You'll never satisfy her.'

'Perhaps,' he'd replied with perfect middle-class poise, 'but at least I won't kill her.'

He remembers how radiant SHE had looked.

(4) He remembers the day SHE found out SHE was pregnant.

SHE hadn't called him at work or jumped into his arms the minute he walked in. That wasn't HER way. SHE'd left the stick on the floor of the bathroom, right there in the middle where it couldn't be missed, and he'd picked it up on his way in like SHE knew he would. That was HER way.

'Why aren't you more excited?' SHE'd asked later that evening.

'I am, I am,' he'd said. 'Of course I am. It's just... I was just... you know, I didn't expect it to happen so quickly... after we... you know... decided to try.'

'But... that's a good thing, isn't it?'

'Yes, yes, of course. It's just... I've got used to us.'

SHE had held him then, and there was so much love in HER touch, in HER eyes.

'But baby,' SHE said, 'there'll always be us.'

Barthes

'If I had to create a god, I would lend him a "slow understanding": a kind of drip-by-drip understanding of problems. People who understand quickly frighten me.'[79]

Him

Thirty days since he's moved out.

He's living in a rented room in Shoreditch above a studio that is let out for various artistic endeavours. By now, he knows the schedule off by heart. On Mondays at six, there is an adult tap class. Tap-tap-clippety-clop. He can hear it through the flimsy floorboards, every tap, every clip, every clop. On Tuesday and Thursday nights at eight, there is a jazz session. The saxophonist and the drummer are always there. Sometimes he hears the bassist, sometimes not, but that could just be the nature of the bass, supportive, subtle, essential.

The jazz is going on now. All three are present today. These are young musicians, he can tell, still finding their way, a kind of groping.

Right now, it's a competition of voices. Like one of Shakespeare's plays.

If they manage to get it right eventually, there will be one voice. The third person. Like Shakespeare himself. Everything is everyone is anything is anyone. There is no 'I' in jazz, like there is no 'I' in Shakespeare.

He looks forward to that time.

On the window directly across from his own window is a printed advertisement for residential accommodation. 'Shared room. To let. Single women only. Minimum six-month rent. En suite. Private. Negotiable.'

Which bit, he wonders, is negotiable?

Just below the negotiable room, on street level, is a KFC, only the K is for Khan's, not Kentucky. 'Fresh Cheap Fried Chicken', the backlit, laminated rooster promises, presumably about itself. The gesture of spontaneous self-sacrifice mildly stokes his interest. He decides to give it a go.

Barthes

'I pass lightly through the reactionary darkness.'[80]

Him

Occasionally on the nights when sleep doesn't come, he goes to an establishment around the corner that generously offers 'Happy Hour, Every Hour', duly disclaimed by some 'Terms and Conditions', in smaller print, which he doesn't bother to read at all.

'You could think ovit as a very twisted poker game, mate,' the bartender explains after he's patronised the place enough times to claim a mutual acquaintanceship if not friendship, 'if life wuz set up like that, I mean, as if it wuz a card game, with winners and losers. Farkit, you wuz dealt the worst farking hand that any player could be dealt.'

He takes a sip of the cold, bitter brew, polishes off the last of the peanuts (roasted, salted).

The bartender shrugs his shoulders, wipes the very top of his bald, pink scalp with the back of his palm, pours him another drink, replenishes the nuts.

'And you did wot? Wot anyone would do, mate, wot anyone would do. You folded.'

Very good, he thinks of the bartender's analysis of his situation, for a man he has known for forty-two days, very, very farking good.

Barthes

'This would be the structure of the "successful" couple: a little prohibition, a good deal of play; to designate desire and then to leave it alone, like those obliging natives who show you the path but don't insist on accompanying you on your way.'[81]

Him

This week there's a pianist. He can hear the notes floating up through the floorboards. Soaring all the way to the ceiling. It is incredible, the difference; the pianist arrives, and the music changes, and now everything is sensuous and sweeping and splendid.

Barthes

'I am either lacerated or ill at ease
and occasionally subject to gusts of life'[82]

Him

The unknown pianist becomes a kind of poetic muse. He has a gift, this pianist, something non-verbal, unconsidered, opening up a kind of possibility in one's mind. His sound is delicate, crystalline.

Upstairs, in the tiny, rented room, he doodles.

We are never done... (he writes). *We are continually creating ourselves. Crafting ourselves, painting ourselves, writing ourselves, weaving ourselves, shaping ourselves, tuning ourselves, strumming ourselves. We are artists of ourselves. We are storytellers of ourselves. We are writers of ourselves. We are poets of ourselves. We are pianists of ourselves.*

He reads his doodle out loud to the accompaniment of the piano.

To him, this music is like the sky. It fills some of the emptiness he has carried around inside him since the summer of 1965 when he discovered his mother's naked body hanging from the ceiling fan of her bedroom; it fills some of that emptiness that SHE could never fill for him, and he could never fill for HER, that they still carry around inside them, but the piano player does, he fills it with the music that he plays, because unbeknownst to him, the piano player carries it, too.

He puts his pen down, reads his words, claps (for himself), then promptly begins to cry.

Barthes

'I utter this strange cry: not: *make it stop!* but: *I want to understand* (what is happening to me)!'[83]

Him

He makes a phone call.

'I'm ready,' he announces, and his voice is surprisingly self-assured. Surprising to himself, that is.

'How are you?' his once Liverpudlian, now St John's Wood-based, Director of the English and Modern Languages Department asks, and he knows he must not mistake the question as one that is asked only out of politeness.

It is a very, very difficult question to answer. Also, slightly farcical.

It requires some creative imagination. Also, a bit of humour.

He says: 'The lunatic, the lover and the poet are of imagination all compact.'

This elicits a laugh.

There's a pause, awkward even in its brevity.

He is being sussed out, he knows that. There are reputations at stake. Wheels in motion, important wheels travelling to grand destinations, and he a mere cog.

'How is...?' The director takes his wife's name. 'We've been, you know, Eileen in particular has been very concerned...' He takes his own wife's name, for whom *he* knows SHE harbours no reciprocal concern. In fact, once when they were on their way home after a particularly arduous dinner party hosted by the director's wife, SHE'd sat in the car, slipped off HER heels one by one, turned to him and said, 'God, that woman is such an insufferable bore, two large boobfuls of pretentious stuff and nonsense.' Even then, he hadn't in good conscience been able to dispute that assessment.

'She wanted to call, you know...' the director is saying now. 'But she thought perhaps it was still too soon.'

'It is too boob,' he says.

'Sorry?'

Jesus fuck.

'Soon, soon, too *soon*, I mean, it might still be a little too... yes, maybe another week. Yes, definitely another week would not be a little too uh *soon*.'

There is another pause. He shakes his head in contempt of himself. Idiot. Complete idiot. Inspired in idiocy.

But then the director says, 'One week, then. I'll let Eileen know.'

And then he continues, in the same breath, 'But you. You are quite sure...?'

'I'm quite sure,' he says.

'There's really no need to rush.'

'I'm not rushing.'

'Your position is completely secure.'

No one's position, he wants to say, is ever secure.

'Thank you,' he says.

'We understand, you know. Everyone. All of us here, we deeply commiserate.'

'Thank you,' he says again.

The director clears his throat. 'You should know,' he says, 'that we have missed you. The students too. At this thing you do, there is no one quite like you.'

Wow, he thinks, that's so poetic, it's fucked-up.

He says: 'Thank you. Thank you, that's very kind.'

'See you then. Monday week?'

'Monday week.' He nods and hangs up.

In the flat across the street, a restless baby cries in its cot. It is brand new, this baby, days old. Even up to a week ago, it simply didn't exist. And now, it asserts its place in the world, it makes its existence known. Life, it has learned (already!), is a matter of survival.

'I know,' he sighs, peering out of the window. 'I know just how you feel.'

He is ready.

Barthes

'Issues/outcomes: Enticement of solutions whatever they may be, which afford the amorous subject, despite their frequently catastrophic character, a temporary peace; hallucinatory manipulation of the possible outcomes of the amorous crisis.'[84]

Him

His phone rings. He doesn't answer. He doesn't know what to tell HER. That he misses HER? (He does.) That he's sorry?

(He is.) But for what?

He makes another list. This one is short.

I am sorry (he writes) *for being: (PICK THE BEST ANSWER)*

    (1) a bad son

    (2) a bad husband

    (3) a bad father

    (4) a bad father-of-a-dead-daughter

(But how to be a good father-of-a-dead-daughter? Is there a manual? Will they do a class downstairs? Wednesdays at eight, at the moment, is free.)

(ALSO THINK ABOUT THESE OPTIONS)

For not being at that bus stop?

For letting her die?

Barthes

'It is said that Time soothes mourning – No, Time makes nothing happen; it merely makes the emotivity of mourning pass.'[85]

Him

Meanwhile, in the outside world, the news cycle opens more wounds.

Air strikes. Civilian deaths. Troops. Ultimate sacrifice. Women and children. Violence. More soldiers. Killed in action. Helmand province. Guerrilla warfare. Rumoured weapons of mass destruction. Resurgence. Top ranking militant. 100th serviceman lost. Guns. Bombs. Improvised explosive devices. UN Security forces. Trans-Afghanistan pipeline. Casualties. Growing number. Human toll. Nuclear risk. Unnamed senior Pentagon official. Successful offensive.

Further losses. Mr President. Al-Qaeda. White House. Taliban. Holy war. God Bless America.

Barthes
'Today, information: pulverized, nonhierarchized, dealing with everything: nothing is protected from information and at the same time nothing is open to reflection.'[86]

Him
There goes life. There it goes. In a whistle and a flash.
Rainbow
Sunday lunch
Bottle of wine
Syncopated beat
Heel tap
Car-horn
Funny joke
Suicide bomb
Too late, too fast, too polaroid.

Barthes
'Where there is a wound, there is a subject.'[87]

Him
Three more months. Ninety days now since he left home, give or take. For the last five days SHE's been incessantly trying to call him. He's been ignoring HER calls. It seems the easiest way.
But SHE tries again. And again. And again.
SHE doesn't stop calling.

It's what he has always loved about HER. HER stubbornness. Love-d. Love. He still loves HER. He will always love HER.

It is never about love. It is always about love.

It is Thursday night at eight.

The jazz pianist downstairs is playing some kind of love tune. It is soulful and very beautiful.

It moves him. He answers. (Fucking pianist.)

'Johnny...'

Johnny. SHE hasn't called him that since *she* died.

'Johnny, I need us... I mean I'd like us... to go... to go visit her. Together. Will you come with me? I don't want you to ask any questions. We haven't done this... just you and I... not once, not since... And I think she'd want us to. I get the feeling like she's waiting for us, that she can't rest until we do. So I want... I *need*... I need you to come with me. Will you? Please?'

He knows: SHE doesn't do 'want'.

He knows: SHE doesn't do 'need'.

He knows: Because 'wanting' and 'needing' is what SHE has only ever wished for and never ever got.

From him. From anyone. Not ever.

He knows.

SHE's crying.

They agree to meet at the entrance of the cemetery on Saturday at noon.

Two lovers on a date.

Barthes

'We were friends and have become estranged. But this was right, and we do not want to conceal and obscure it from ourselves as if we had reason to feel ashamed. We are two ships each of which has its goal and course; our paths may cross and we may celebrate a feast together, as we did – and then the good ships rested so quietly in one harbour and one sunshine that it may have looked as if they had reached their goal and as if they had one goal. But then the mighty force of our tasks drove us apart again into different seas and sunny zones, and perhaps we shall never see each other again; perhaps we shall meet again but fail to recognize each other: our exposure to different seas and suns has changed us.'[88]

Him
There's a place that they go to seek solace
    Him and HER
    They tell no one
    They twist their way through the grassy paths
    Past the wrought-iron railings
    Past the forest of grass
    Past the yew and the holly and the cedar
    They don't speak
    Lest they awaken the dead
    Lying under centuries-crumbled stone
    Until they arrive
    Beyond the hedgerows
    To that smooth marble sanctuary
    Where their daughter is buried.

And then SHE says, 'Johnny, I want a divorce.'
    And he says, 'Okay.'
    And then he says, 'I loved her with all my life.'

And SHE says, 'I know.'

And maybe, he thinks, maybe that's all he needed to hear. Maybe, he thinks, thank you. Maybe, he thinks, he no longer needs Barthes.

It begins like a children's story.

Once upon a time, there was a family of three
mum
and dad
and daughter

but then she died
and the maths failed

now there is a new cast of characters – a motley crew, this one

ex-mum
and ex-dad
and dead daughter
and ex-husband
and ex-wife
and a dead French theorist
and all that's left of love

and then there were seven.

Acknowledgements

Thank you, Pat Murphy, for living this project with me. It begins and ends with you.

Thanks also to:

Hester Cameron and Jas Johal for being my first readers and more importantly for informing me that you cried. On some level, that means the manuscript worked.

The ever so hardworking team at Fairlight for keeping the faith in me and my work and for making any of this possible. My editors Urška Vidoni and Laura Shanahan, for your indispensable guidance throughout the process.

Sharon Rubin for painstakingly sorting out the permissioning involved in quoting Roland Barthes's work and to the custodians of these texts for kindly granting us permission.

To the late Roland Barthes himself – intellectual giant, underappreciated genius, my muse.

My two boys, Ranbir and Reyaan, for filling my non-writing life with so much joy; it allows my writing life to continue.

My greatest thanks, as ever, is to Sid, for pretty much everything else.

Notes

[1] Barthes, R. (1977–1979). *Mourning Diary*, trans. Richard Howard, annotated edition. New York: Macmillan, 2012.

[2] Barthes, R. (1957). *Mythologies*, trans. Annette Lavers, revised edition. London: Vintage Classics, 2009.

[3] Barthes, R. (1977–1979). *Mourning Diary*, trans. Richard Howard, annotated edition. New York: Macmillan, 2012.

[4] Barthes, R. (1977). *A Lover's Discourse: Fragments*, trans. Richard Howard. London: Vintage Classics, 2018.

[5] Barthes, R. (1977). *A Lover's Discourse: Fragments*, trans. Richard Howard. London: Vintage Classics, 2018.

[6] Barthes, R. (1957). *Mythologies*, trans. Annette Lavers, revised edition. London: Vintage Classics, 2009.

[7] Barthes, R. (1977). *A Lover's Discourse: Fragments*, trans. Richard Howard. London: Vintage Classics, 2018.

[8] Barthes, R. (1977–1979). *Mourning Diary*, trans. Richard Howard, annotated edition. New York: Macmillan, 2012.

[9] Barthes, R. (1977). *A Lover's Discourse: Fragments*, trans. Richard Howard. London: Vintage Classics, 2018.

[10] Barthes, R. (1957). *Mythologies*, trans. Annette Lavers, revised edition. London: Vintage Classics, 2009.

[11] Barthes, R. (1977–1979). *Mourning Diary*, trans. Richard Howard, annotated edition. New York: Macmillan, 2012.

[12] Barthes, R. (1977–1979). *Mourning Diary*, trans. Richard Howard, annotated edition. New York: Macmillan, 2012.

[13] Barthes, R. (1977). *A Lover's Discourse: Fragments*, trans. Richard Howard. London: Vintage Classics, 2018.

[14] Barthes, R. (1977–1979). *Mourning Diary*, trans. Richard Howard, annotated edition. New York: Macmillan, 2012.

¹⁵ Barthes, R. (1975). *Roland Barthes by Roland Barthes*, trans. Richard Howard. Berkeley: Macmillan, 2010.

¹⁶ Barthes, R. *A Barthes Reader*, selection and introduction by Susan Sontag. New York: Hill and Wang, 1982.

¹⁷ Barthes, R. (1973). *The Pleasure of the Text*, trans. Richard Miller. New York: Hill and Wang, 1975.

¹⁸ Barthes, R. (1977). *A Lover's Discourse: Fragments*, trans. Richard Howard. London: Vintage Classics, 2018.

¹⁹ Barthes, R. (1975). *Roland Barthes by Roland Barthes*, trans. Richard Howard. Berkeley: Macmillan, 2010.

²⁰ Barthes, R. (1968). *Writing Degree Zero*, trans. Annette Lavers. New York: Hill and Wang, 2012.

²¹ Barthes, R. (1977). *A Lover's Discourse: Fragments*, trans. Richard Howard. London: Vintage Classics, 2018.

²² Barthes, R. (1977–1979). *Mourning Diary*, trans. Richard Howard, annotated edition. New York: Macmillan, 2012.

²³ Barthes, R. (1977). *A Lover's Discourse: Fragments*, trans. Richard Howard. London: Vintage Classics, 2018.

²⁴ Barthes, R. (1977–1979). *Mourning Diary*, trans. Richard Howard, annotated edition. New York: Macmillan, 2012.

²⁵ Barthes, R. (1957). *Mythologies*, trans. Annette Lavers, revised edition. London: Vintage Classics, 2009.

²⁶ Barthes, R. (1977–1979). *Mourning Diary*, trans. Richard Howard, annotated edition. New York: Macmillan, 2012.

²⁷ Barthes, R. (1980). *Camera Lucida: Reflections on Photography*, trans. Richard Howard. London: Vintage Classics, 1981.

²⁸ Barthes, R. (1977). *A Lover's Discourse: Fragments*, trans. Richard Howard. London: Vintage Classics, 2018.

²⁹ Barthes, R. (1977). *A Lover's Discourse: Fragments*, trans. Richard Howard. London: Vintage Classics, 2018.

[30] Barthes, R. (1977). *A Lover's Discourse: Fragments*, trans. Richard Howard. London: Vintage Classics, 2018.

[31] Barthes, R. (1977). *A Lover's Discourse: Fragments*, trans. Richard Howard. London: Vintage Classics, 2018.

[32] Barthes, R. (1977). 'Inaugural Lecture', *A Barthes Reader*, selection and introduction by Susan Sontag. New York: Hill and Wang, 1982.

[33] Barthes, R. (1977–1979). *Mourning Diary*, trans. Richard Howard, annotated edition. New York: Macmillan, 2012.

[34] Barthes, R. (1977). *A Lover's Discourse: Fragments*, trans. Richard Howard. London: Vintage Classics, 2018.

[35] Barthes, R. (1977). *A Lover's Discourse: Fragments*, trans. Richard Howard. London: Vintage Classics, 2018.

[36] Barthes, R. (1977–1979). *Mourning Diary*, trans. Richard Howard, annotated edition. New York: Macmillan, 2012.

[37] Barthes, R. (1977). *A Lover's Discourse: Fragments*, trans. Richard Howard. London: Vintage Classics, 2018.

[38] Barthes, R. (1977–1979). *Mourning Diary*, trans. Richard Howard, annotated edition. New York: Macmillan, 2012.

[39] Barthes, R. (1973). *The Pleasure of the Text*, trans. Richard Miller. New York: Hill and Wang, 1975.

[40] Barthes, R. (1977). *A Lover's Discourse: Fragments*, trans. Richard Howard. London: Vintage Classics, 2018.

[41] Barthes, R. (1977). *A Lover's Discourse: Fragments*, trans. Richard Howard. London: Vintage Classics, 2018.

[42] Barthes, R. (1980). *Camera Lucida: Reflections on Photography*, trans. Richard Howard. London: Vintage Classics, 1981.

[43] Barthes, R. (1973). *The Pleasure of the Text*, trans. Richard Miller. New York: Hill and Wang, 1975.

[44] Barthes, R. (1957). *Mythologies*, trans. Annette Lavers, revised edition. London: Vintage Classics, 2009.

45 Barthes, R. (1977–1979). *Mourning Diary*, trans. Richard Howard, annotated edition. New York: Macmillan, 2012.

46 Barthes, R. (1980). *Camera Lucida: Reflections on Photography*, trans. Richard Howard. London: Vintage Classics, 1981.

47 Barthes, R. (1977). *A Lover's Discourse: Fragments*, trans. Richard Howard. London: Vintage Classics, 2018.

48 Barthes, R. (1977–1979). *Mourning Diary*, trans. Richard Howard, annotated edition. New York: Macmillan, 2012.

49 Barthes, R. (1957). 'The Face of Garbo', *Mythologies*, trans. Annette Lavers, revised edition. London: Vintage Classics, 2009.

50 Barthes, R. (1977). *A Lover's Discourse: Fragments*, trans. Richard Howard. London: Vintage Classics, 2018.

51 Barthes, R. (1977). *A Lover's Discourse: Fragments*, trans. Richard Howard. London: Vintage Classics, 2018.

52 Barthes, R. (1977–1979). *Mourning Diary*, trans. Richard Howard, annotated edition. New York: Macmillan, 2012.

53 Barthes, R. (1977–1979). *Mourning Diary*, trans. Richard Howard, annotated edition. New York: Macmillan, 2012.

54 Barthes, R. (1977–1979). *Mourning Diary*, trans. Richard Howard, annotated edition. New York: Macmillan, 2012.

55 Barthes, R. (1977). *A Lover's Discourse: Fragments*, trans. Richard Howard. London: Vintage Classics, 2018.

56 Barthes, R. (1977–1979). *Mourning Diary*, trans. Richard Howard, annotated edition. New York: Macmillan, 2012.

57 Barthes, R. (1977). *A Lover's Discourse: Fragments*, trans. Richard Howard. London: Vintage Classics, 2018.

58 Barthes, R. (1977–1979). *Mourning Diary*, trans. Richard Howard, annotated edition. New York: Macmillan, 2012.

59 Barthes, R. (1977). *A Lover's Discourse: Fragments*, trans. Richard Howard. London: Vintage Classics, 2018.

[60] Barthes, R. (1977). *A Lover's Discourse: Fragments*, trans. Richard Howard. London: Vintage Classics, 2018.

[61] Barthes, R. (1977). *A Lover's Discourse: Fragments*, trans. Richard Howard. London: Vintage Classics, 2018.

[62] Barthes, R. (1977). *A Lover's Discourse: Fragments*, trans. Richard Howard. London: Vintage Classics, 2018.

[63] Barthes, R. (1977–1979). *Mourning Diary*, trans. Richard Howard, annotated edition. New York: Macmillan, 2012.

[64] Barthes, R. (1977). *A Lover's Discourse: Fragments*, trans. Richard Howard. London: Vintage Classics, 2018.

[65] Barthes, R. (1977). *A Lover's Discourse: Fragments*, trans. Richard Howard. London: Vintage Classics, 2018.

[66] Barthes, R. (1977). *A Lover's Discourse: Fragments*, trans. Richard Howard. London: Vintage Classics, 2018.

[67] Barthes, R. (1977–1979). *Mourning Diary*, trans. Richard Howard, annotated edition. New York: Macmillan, 2012.

[68] Barthes, R. (1977). *A Lover's Discourse: Fragments*, trans. Richard Howard. London: Vintage Classics, 2018.

[69] Barthes, R. (1977). *A Lover's Discourse: Fragments*, trans. Richard Howard. London: Vintage Classics, 2018.

[70] Barthes, R. (1977–1979). *Mourning Diary*, trans. Richard Howard, annotated edition. New York: Macmillan, 2012.

[71] Barthes, R. (1973). *The Pleasure of the Text*, trans. Richard Miller. New York: Hill and Wang, 1975.

[72] Barthes, R. (1977). *A Lover's Discourse: Fragments*, trans. Richard Howard. London: Vintage Classics, 2018.

[73] Barthes, R. (1977). *A Lover's Discourse: Fragments*, trans. Richard Howard. London: Vintage Classics, 2018.

[74] Barthes, R. (1977). *A Lover's Discourse: Fragments*, trans. Richard Howard. London: Vintage Classics, 2018.

[75] Barthes, R. (1977). *A Lover's Discourse: Fragments*, trans. Richard Howard. London: Vintage Classics, 2018.

[76] Barthes, R. (1980). *Camera Lucida: Reflections on Photography*, trans. Richard Howard. London: Vintage Classics, 1981.

[77] Barthes, R. (1977). *A Lover's Discourse: Fragments*, trans. Richard Howard. London: Vintage Classics, 2018.

[78] Barthes, R. (1977). *A Lover's Discourse: Fragments*, trans. Richard Howard. London: Vintage Classics, 2018.

[79] Barthes, R. (1977). *The Neutral: Lecture Course at the Collège de France*. New York: Columbia University Press, 2007.

[80] Barthes, R. (1973). *The Pleasure of the Text*, trans. Richard Miller. New York: Hill and Wang, 1975.

[81] Barthes, R. (1977). *A Lover's Discourse: Fragments*, trans. Richard Howard. London: Vintage Classics, 2018.

[82] Barthes, R. (1977–1979). *Mourning Diary*, trans. Richard Howard, annotated edition. New York: Macmillan, 2012.

[83] Barthes, R. (1977). *A Lover's Discourse: Fragments*, trans. Richard Howard. London: Vintage Classics, 2018.

[84] Barthes, R. (1977). *A Lover's Discourse: Fragments*, trans. Richard Howard. London: Vintage Classics, 2018.

[85] Barthes, R. (1977–1979). *Mourning Diary*, trans. Richard Howard, annotated edition. New York: Macmillan, 2012.

[86] Barthes, R. (1977). *The Neutral: Lecture Course at the Collège de France*. New York: Columbia University Press, 2007.

[87] Barthes, R. (1977). *A Lover's Discourse: Fragments*, trans. Richard Howard. London: Vintage Classics, 2018.

[88] Barthes, R. (1977). *A Lover's Discourse: Fragments*, trans. Richard Howard. London: Vintage Classics, 2018.

About the Author

Ami Rao is a British-American writer who was born in Calcutta, India and has lived and worked in New York City, London, Paris, San Francisco and Los Angeles. Ami has a BA in English Literature and Economics from Ohio Wesleyan University and an MBA from Harvard Business School. When she is not reading, writing, cooking, eating, sailing or dancing, she can be found listening to jazz, her 'one great unrequited love'. Ami also mentors girls of colour, with a keen emphasis on the merits of reading and education.

She co-wrote a sports memoir, *Centaur*, which was published in 2017. The book won the General Outstanding Sports Book of the Year Award 2018 and was shortlisted for the William Hill Sports Book of the Year 2017. Her debut novel, *David and Ameena*, was published by Fairlight Books in 2021.

AMI RAO

DAVID AND AMEENA

Modern-day New York, a subway train. David, an American-Jewish jazz musician, torn between his dreams and his parents' expectations, sees a woman across the carriage. Ameena, a British-Pakistani artist who left Manchester to escape the pressure from her conservative family, sees David.

When a moment of sublime beauty occurs unexpectedly, the two connect, moved by their shared experience. From this flows a love that it appears will triumph above all. But as David and Ameena navigate their relationship, their ambitions and the city they love, they discover the external world is not so easy to keep at bay.

Ami Rao's masterful debut novel picks apart the lives of two people, stripping them of their collective identities and, in doing so, facing up to the challenge of today: can love give us the freedom to accept our differences?

'Ami Rao intricately weaves threads of love, family, politics and identity to create a beautiful, and very real, modern love story that sparkles beneath a New York skyline.'
—Huma Qureshi, author of *How We Met*

'I've never read such an accurate and telling evocation of the additional complications of personal creative expression.'
—Tim Hayward, writer, broadcaster and columnist